BENEATH DARKSMITH MANOR, EXPERIMENTING IN
MAD SCIENCE IS BUSINESS AS USUAL.

WHEN BIG BAD EVIL GUYS NEED MINIONS, WHEN LOCAL
TOWNS NEED LEGIONS OF MINDLESS DRONES TO FILE
PAPERWORK, WHEN FESTIVALS NEED AN ARMY OF
DANCING SKELETONS TO SPREAD HOLIDAY CHEER,
DARKSMITH MANOR IS THE FIRST CHOICE IN
DELIVERING THESE DASTARDLY DEEDS.

HOWEVER, SOMETIMES THINGS GO WRONG...

FOR OTHER, MORE OR LESS SUCCESSFUL EXPERIMENTS
IN MAD SCIENCE, VISIT:

WWW.FEARANDSUNSHINE.COM

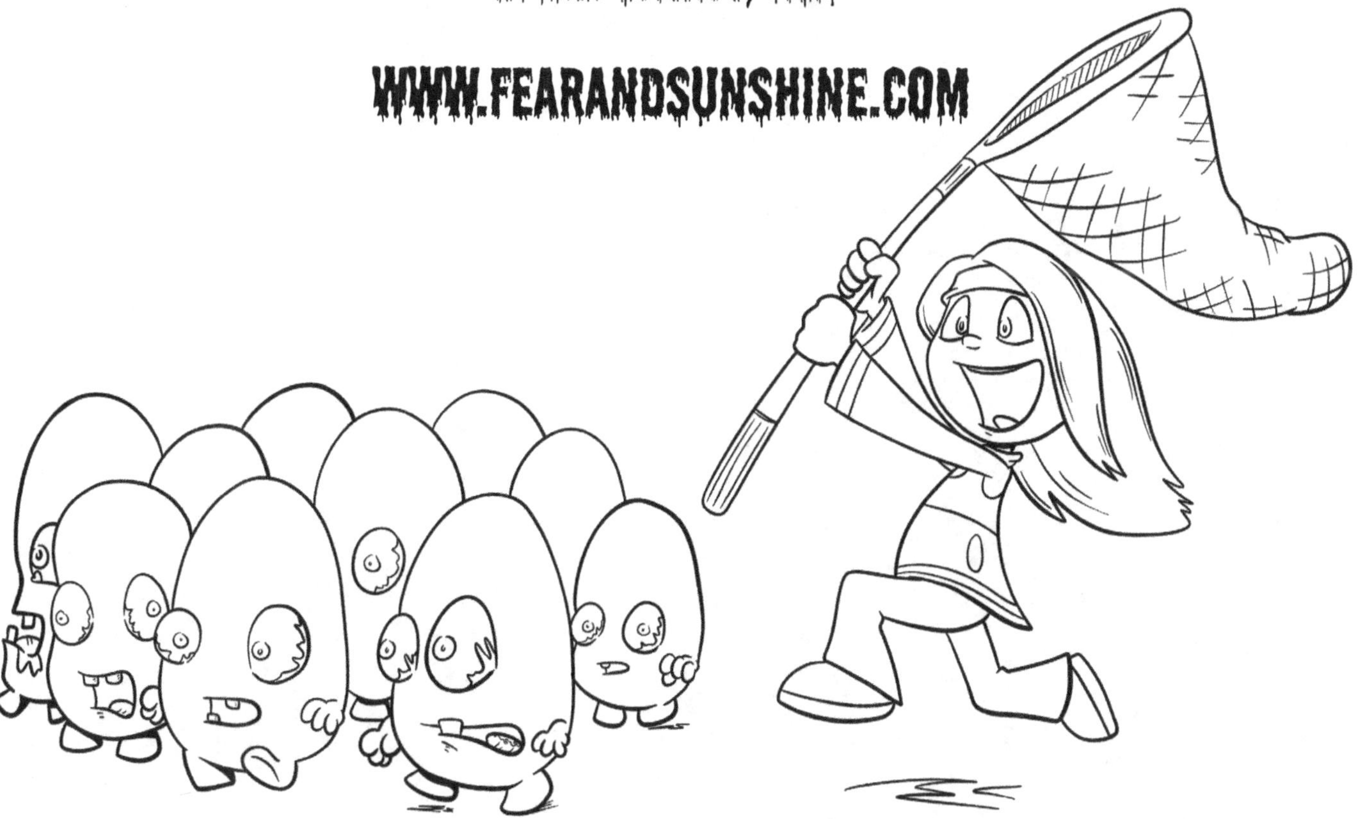

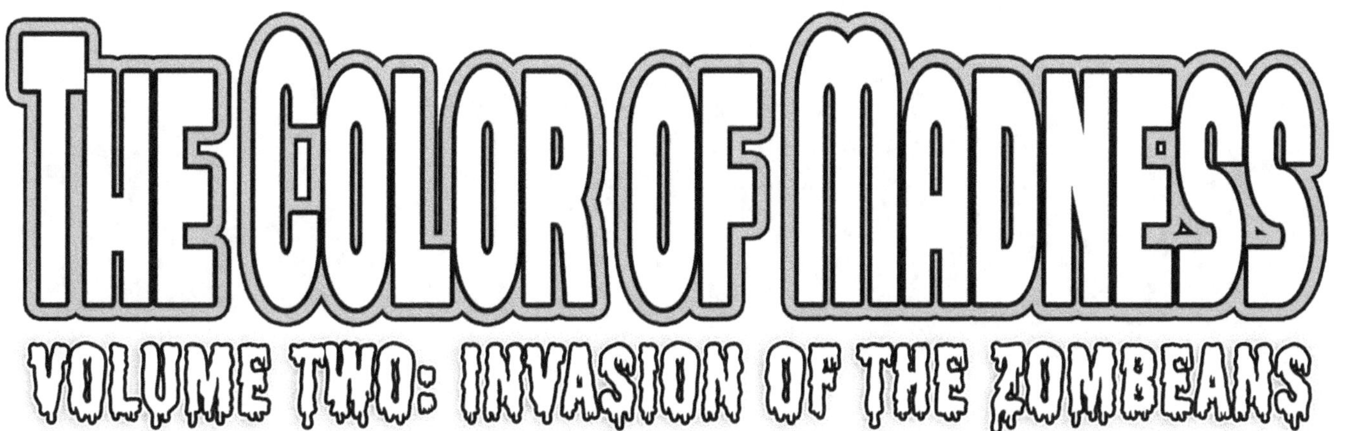

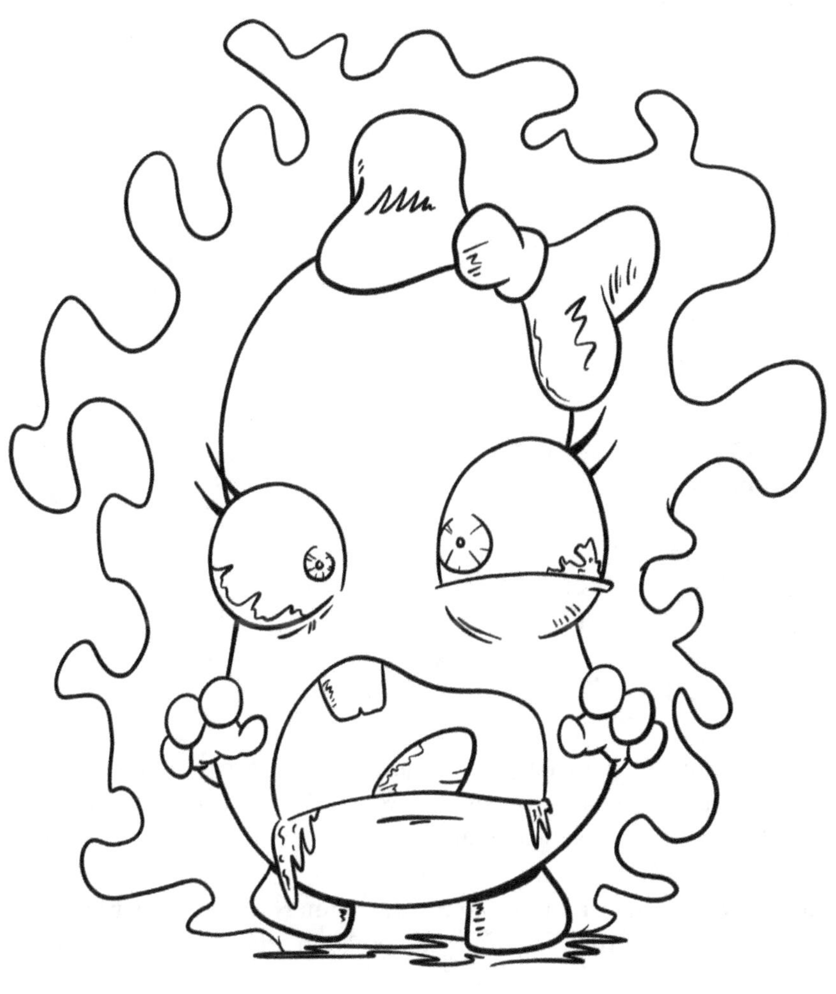

Created by

Donovan Scherer

The Color of Madness: Volume 2
Invasion of the ZomBeans

For information regarding permission, write to:

Studio Moonfall LLC
5031 7th Avenue
Kenosha, WI 53140

ISBN: 978-1-942811-33-6

www.StudioMoonfall.com

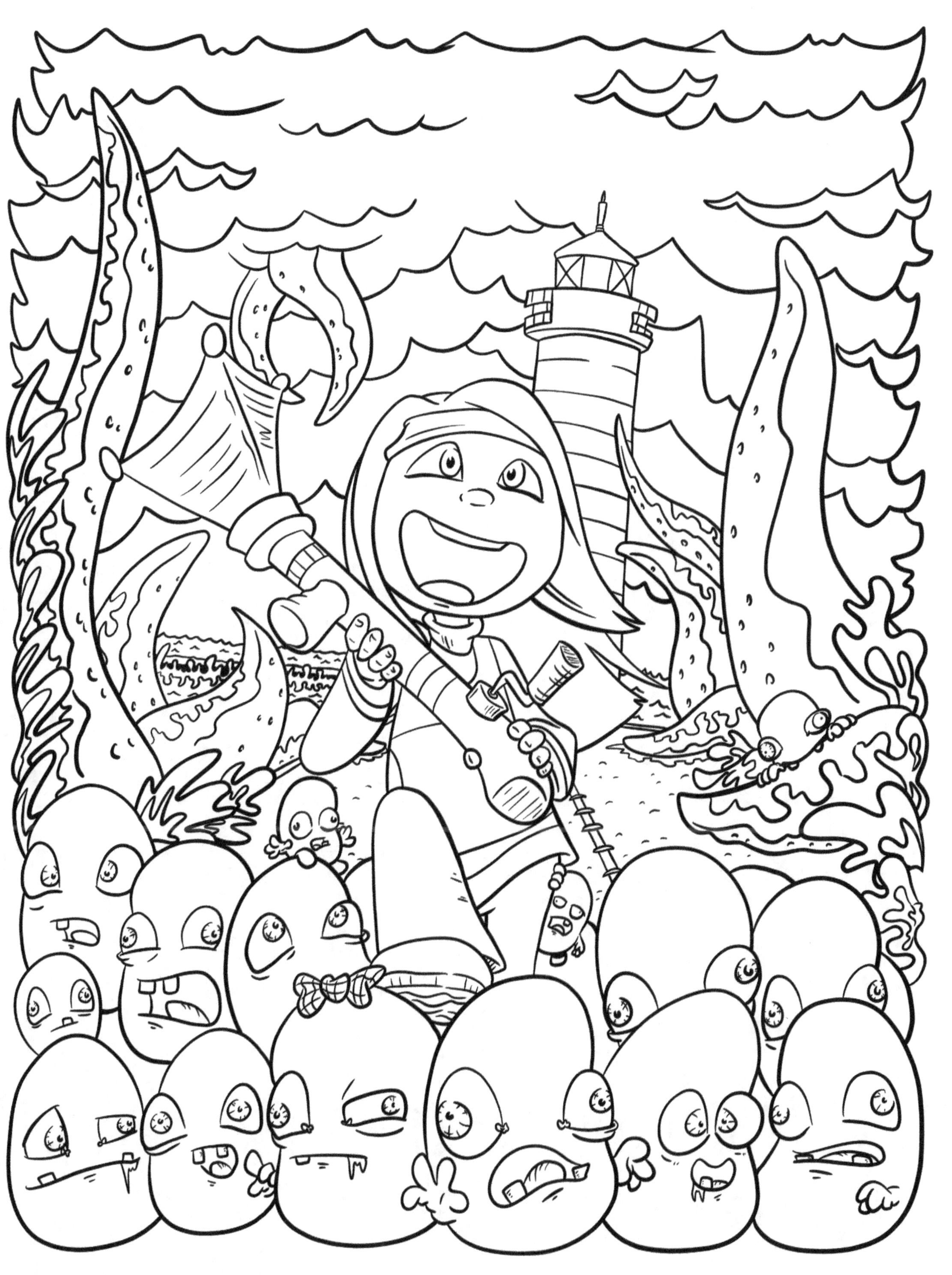

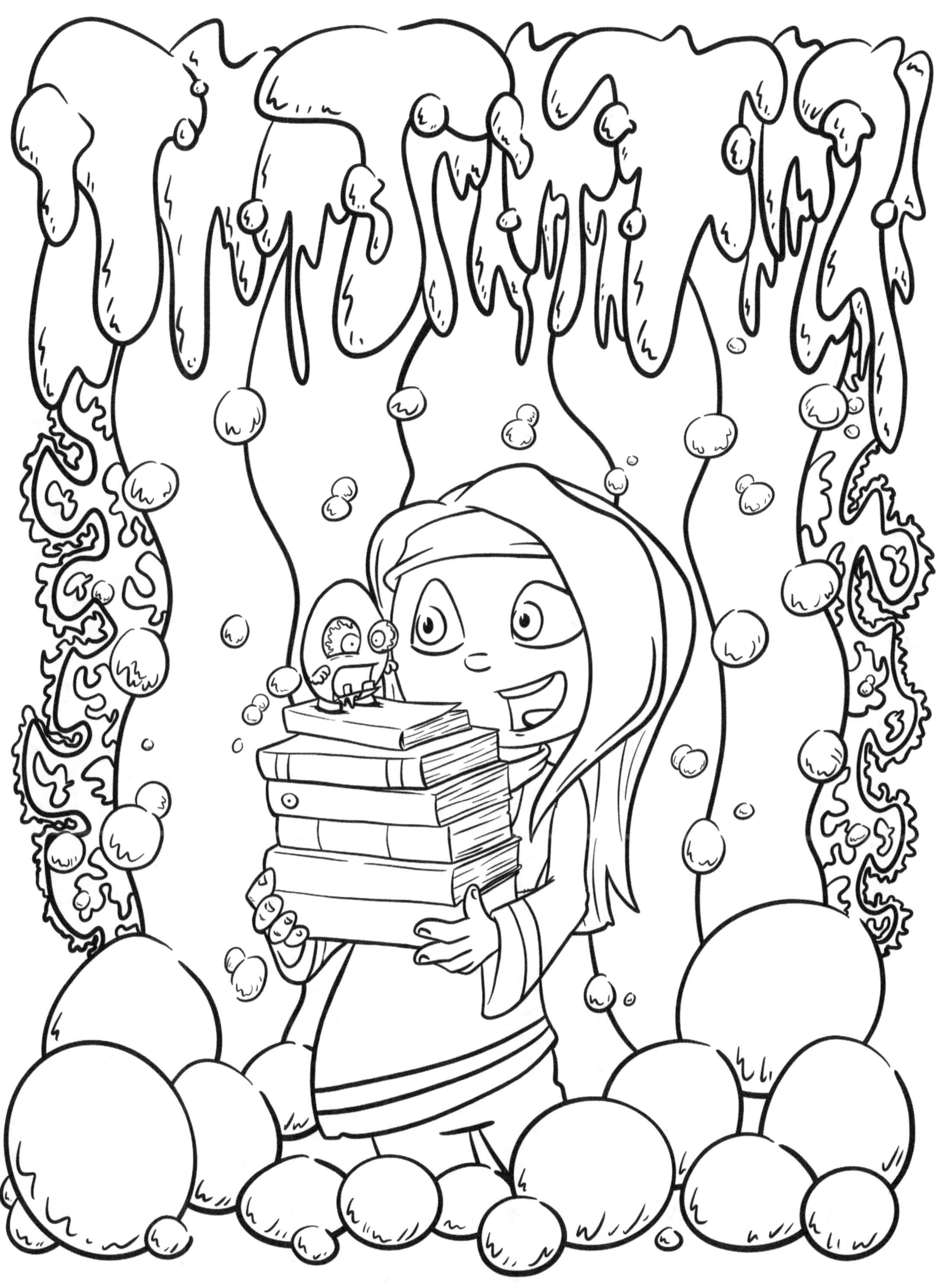

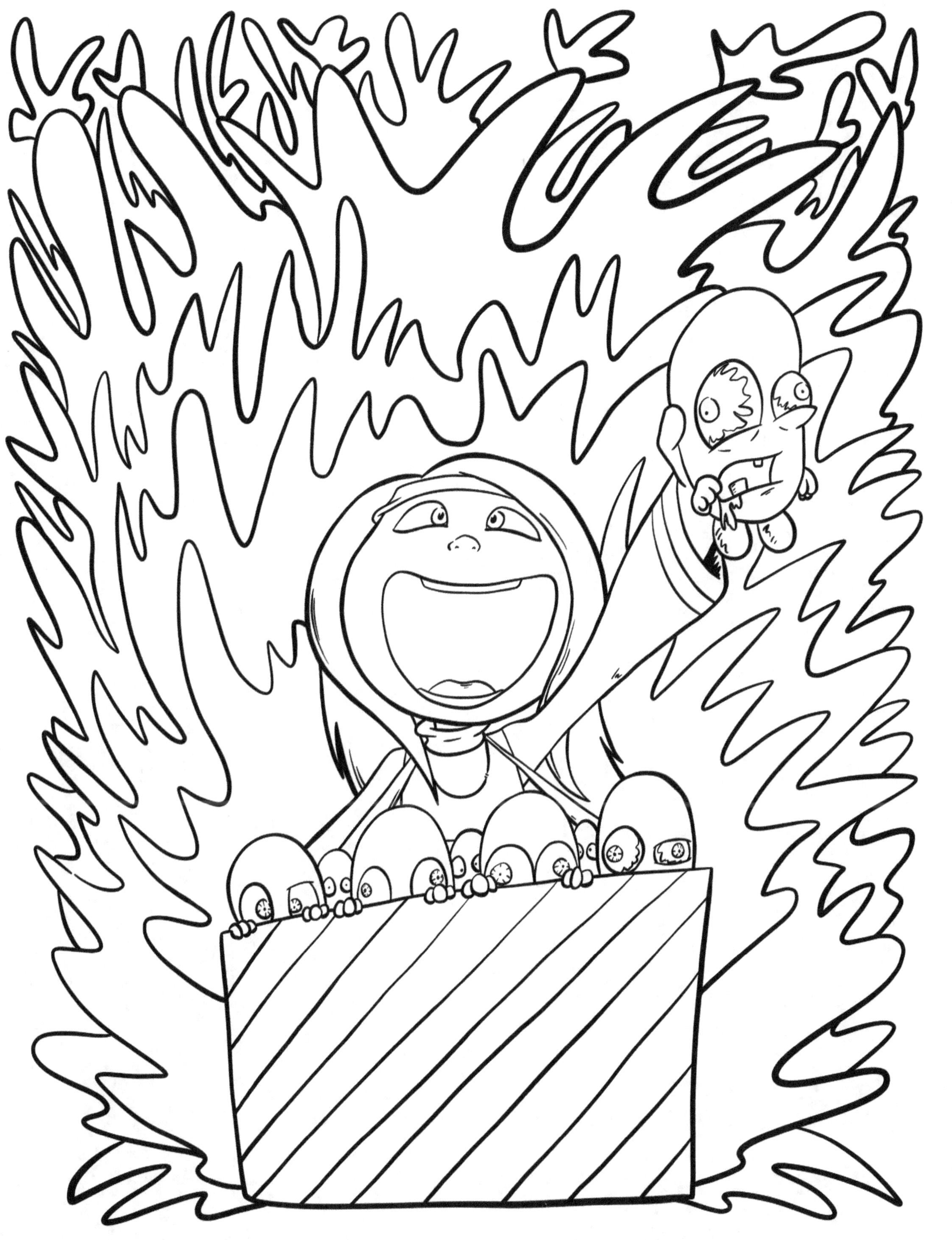

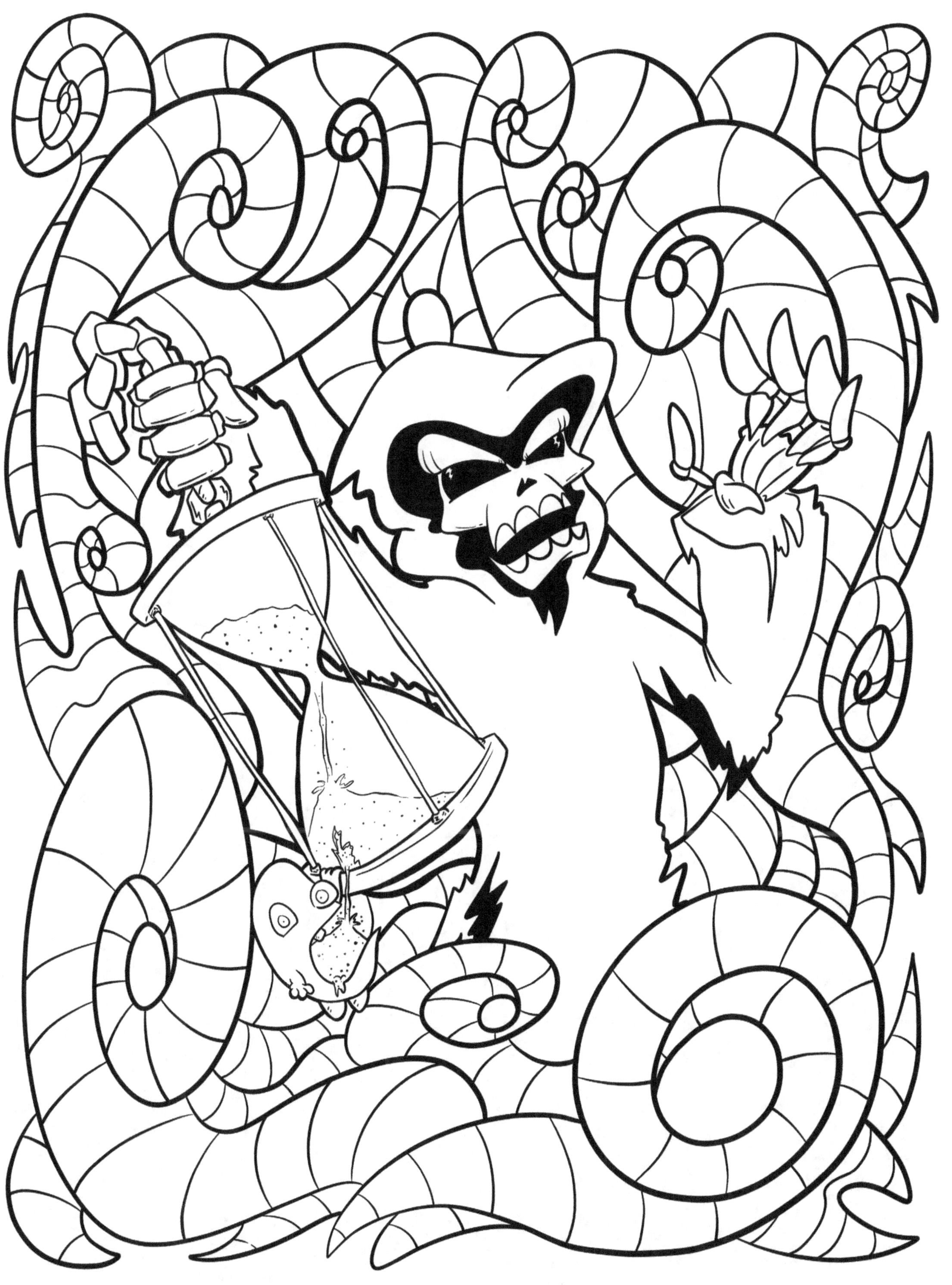

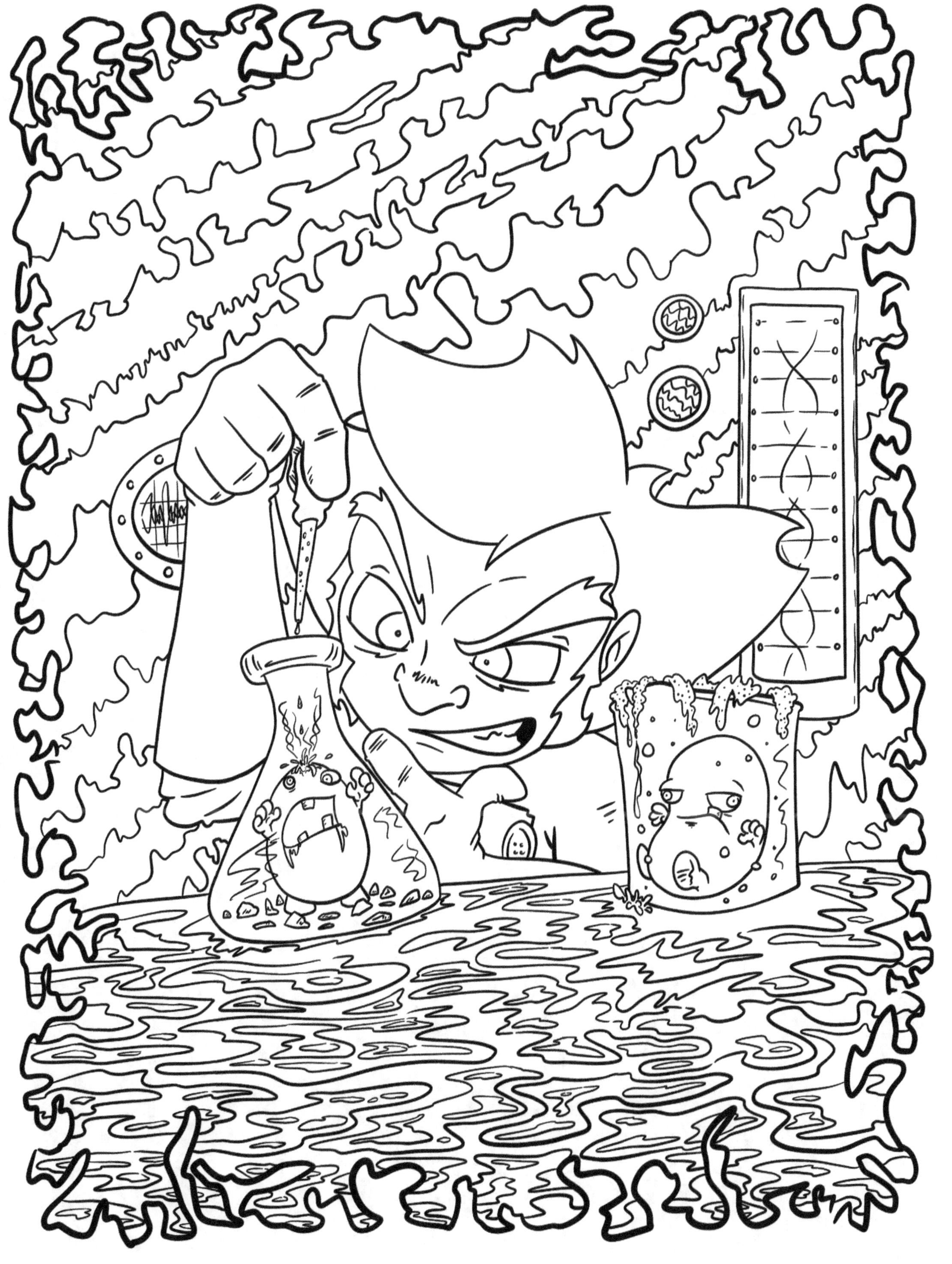

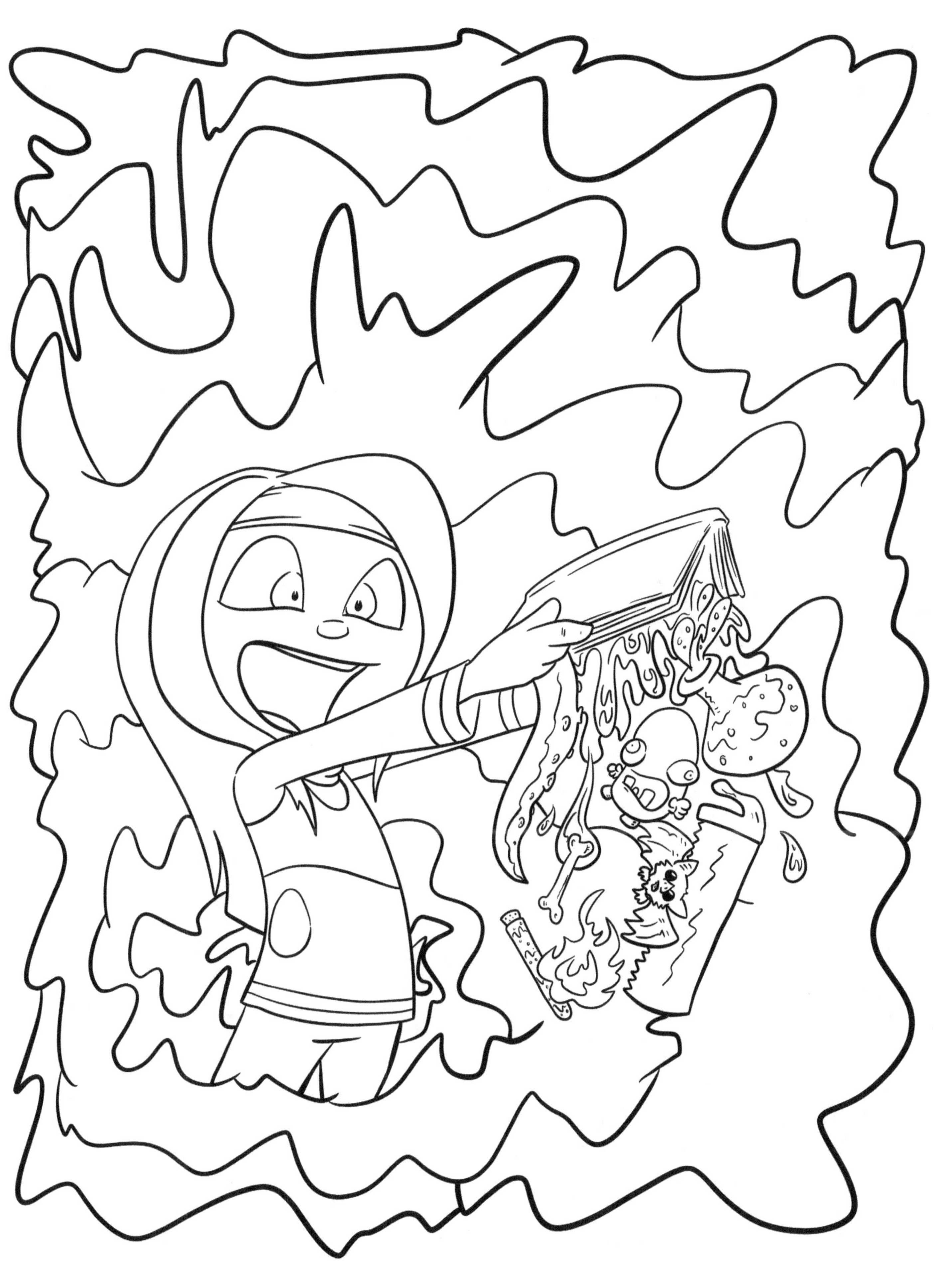

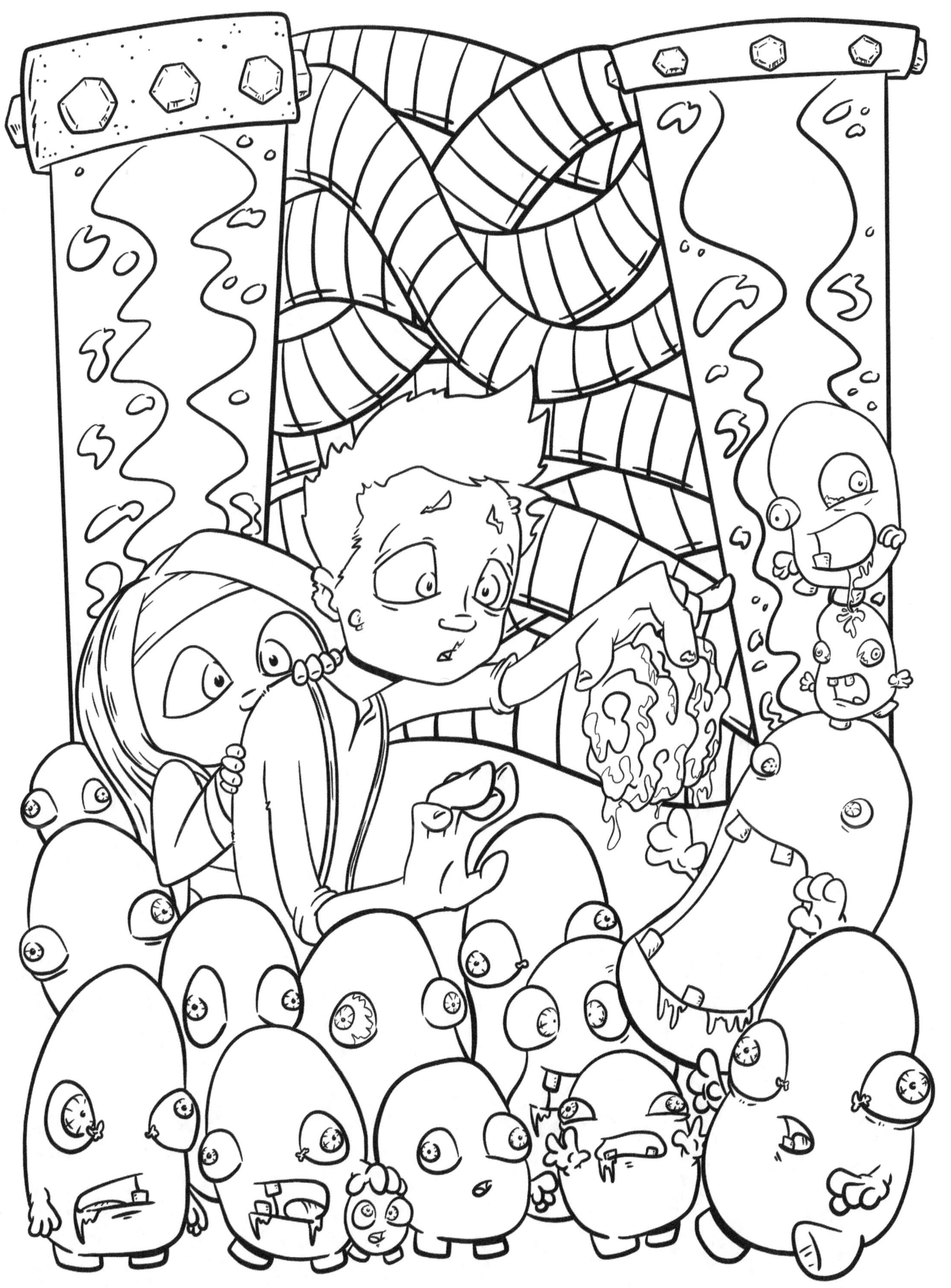

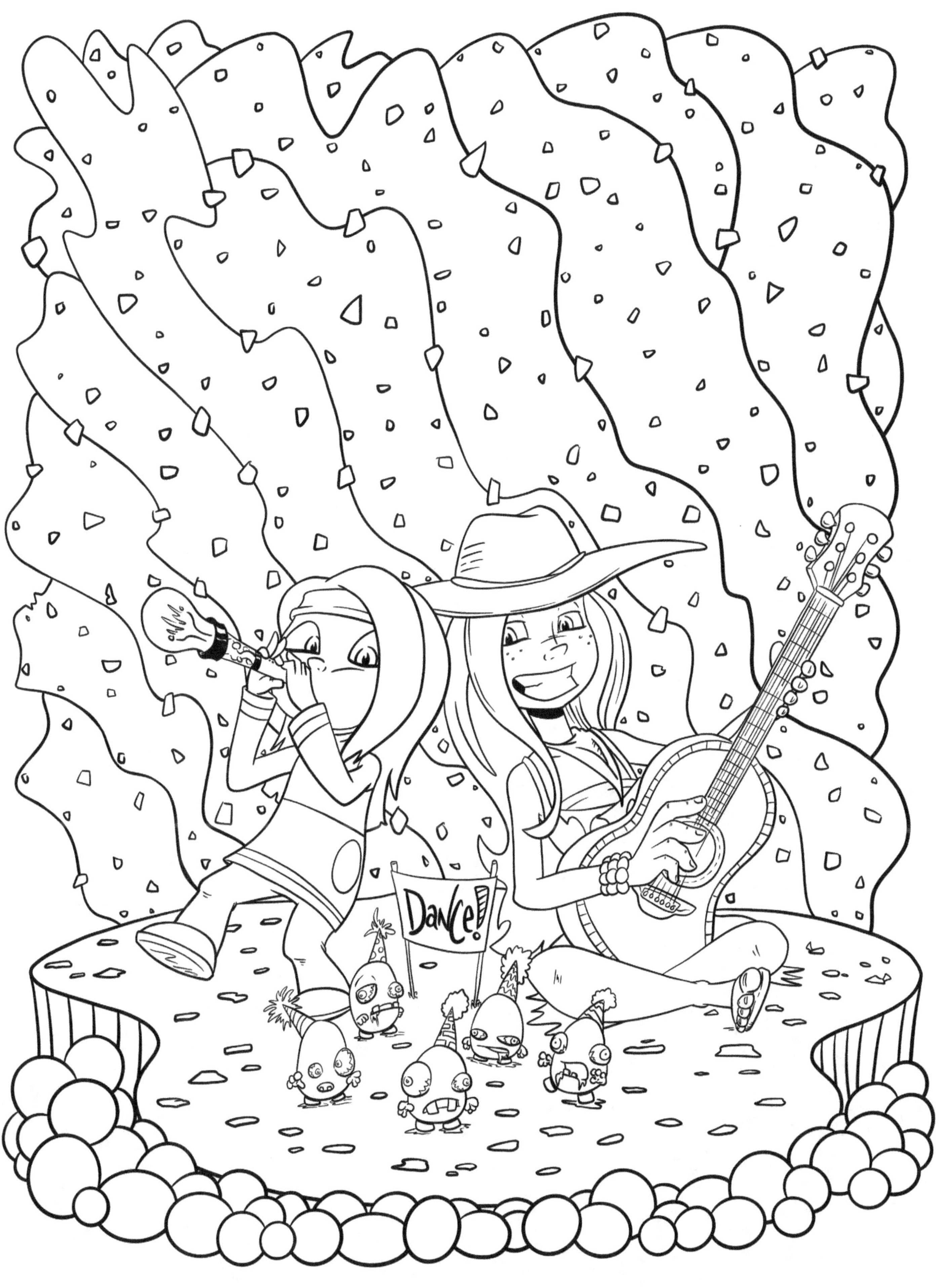

DanCe!

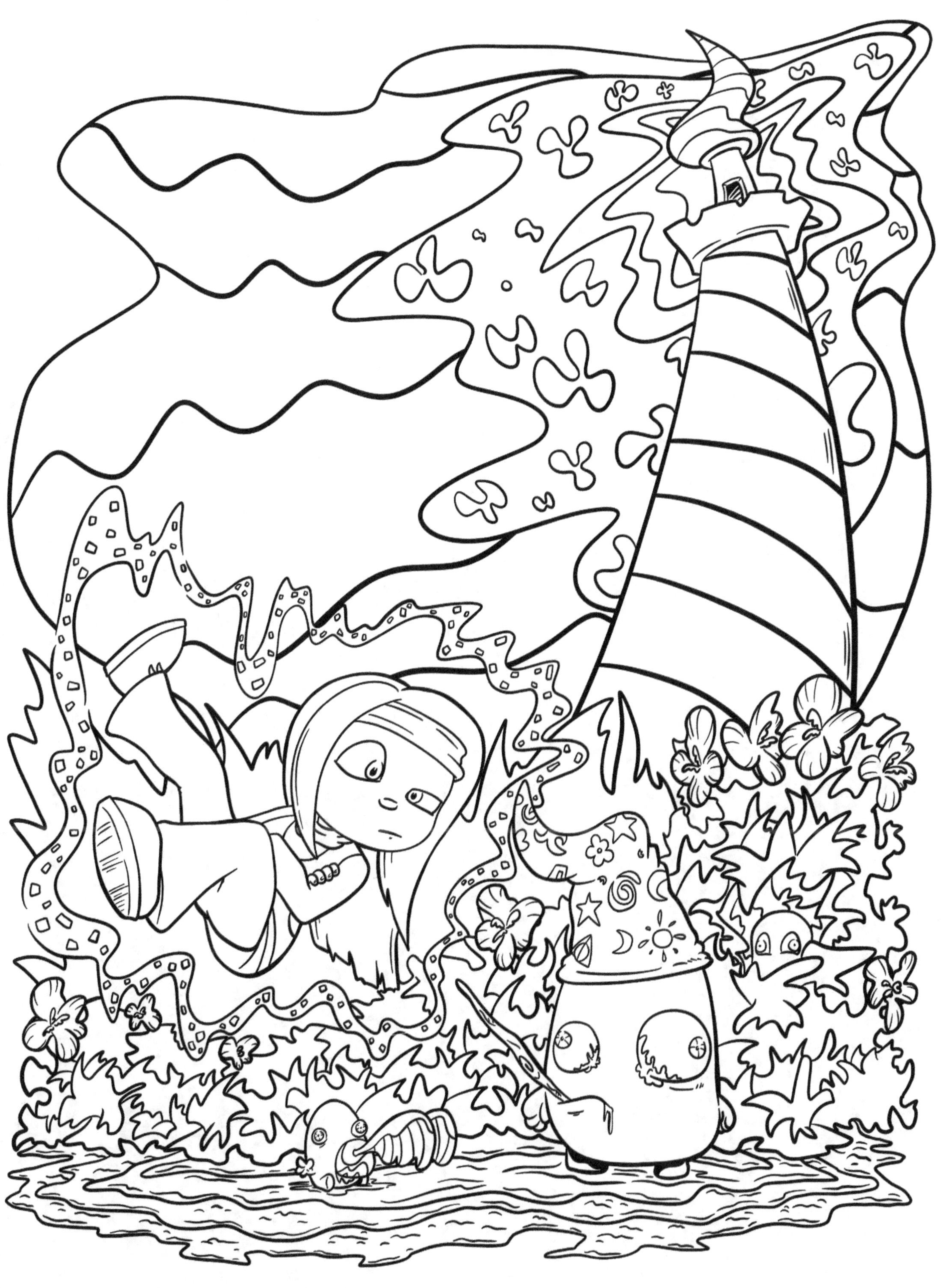

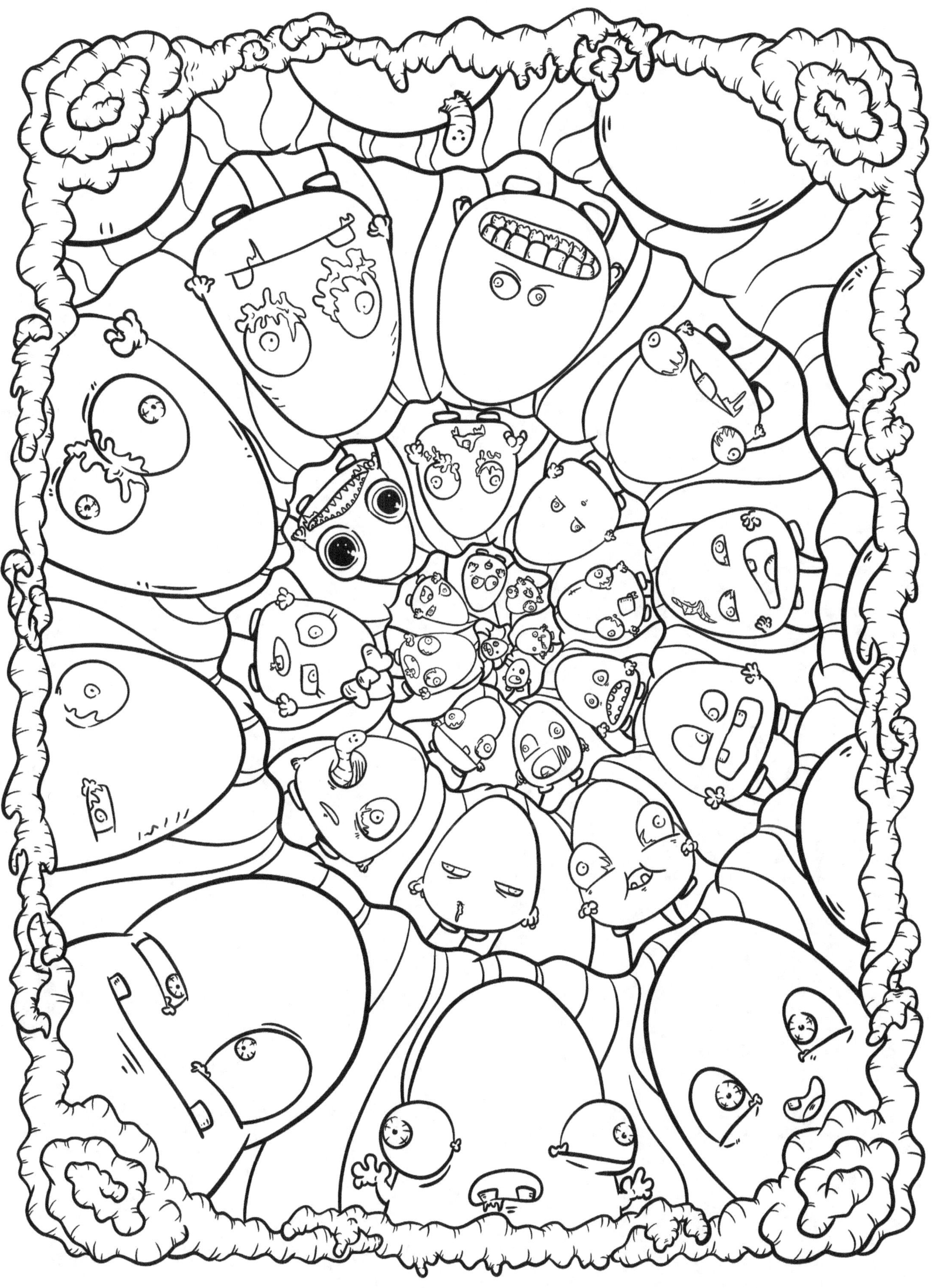

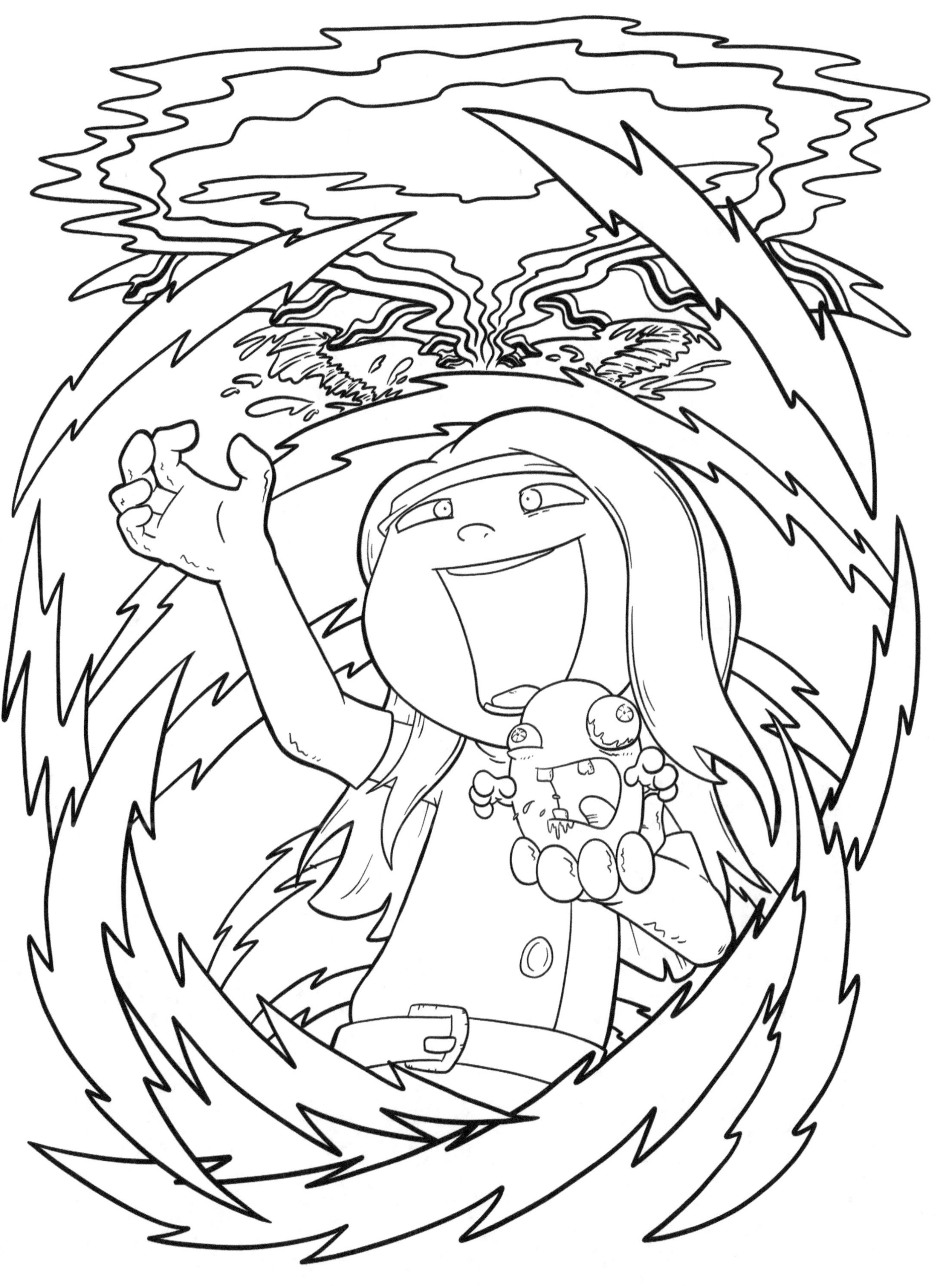

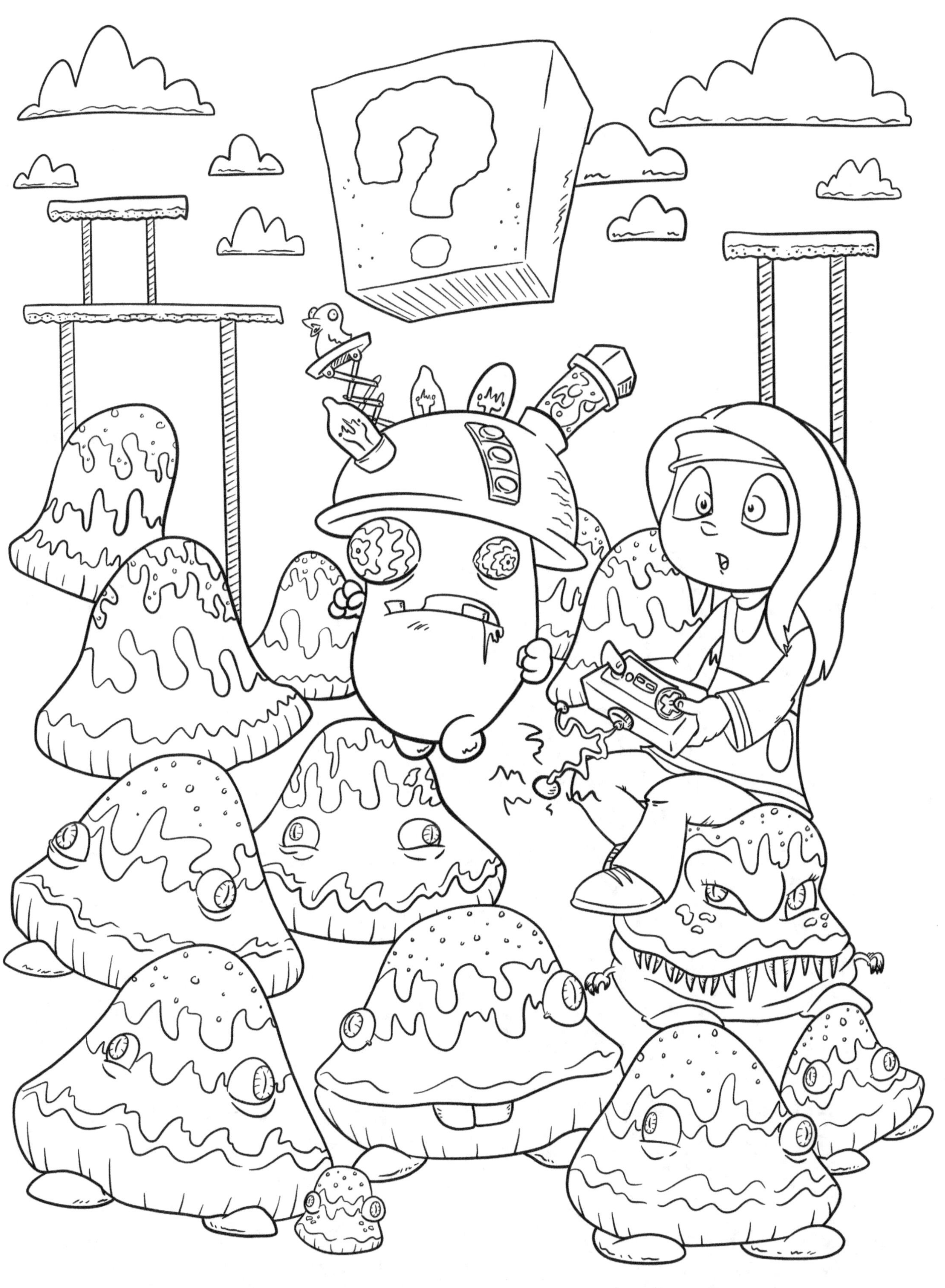

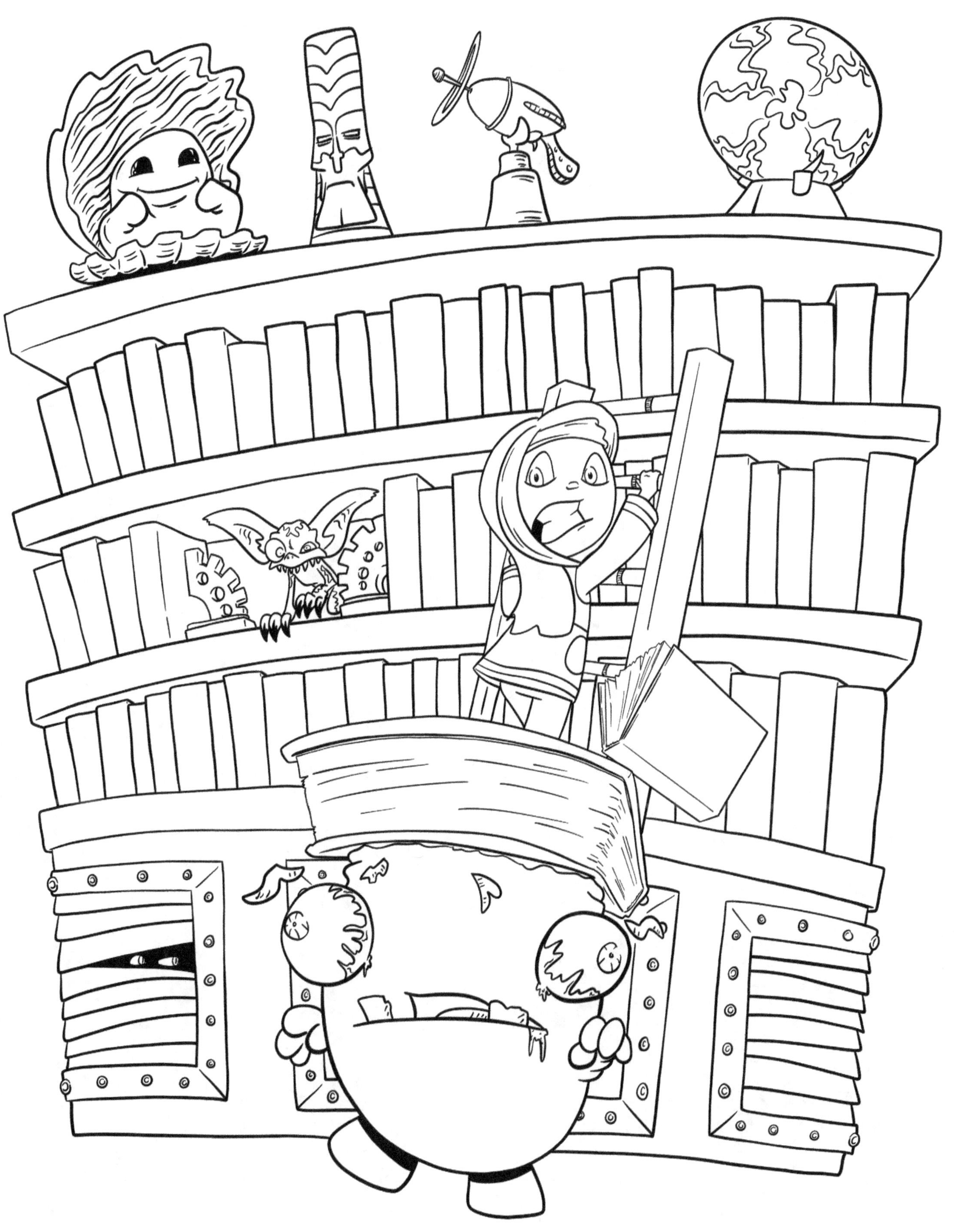

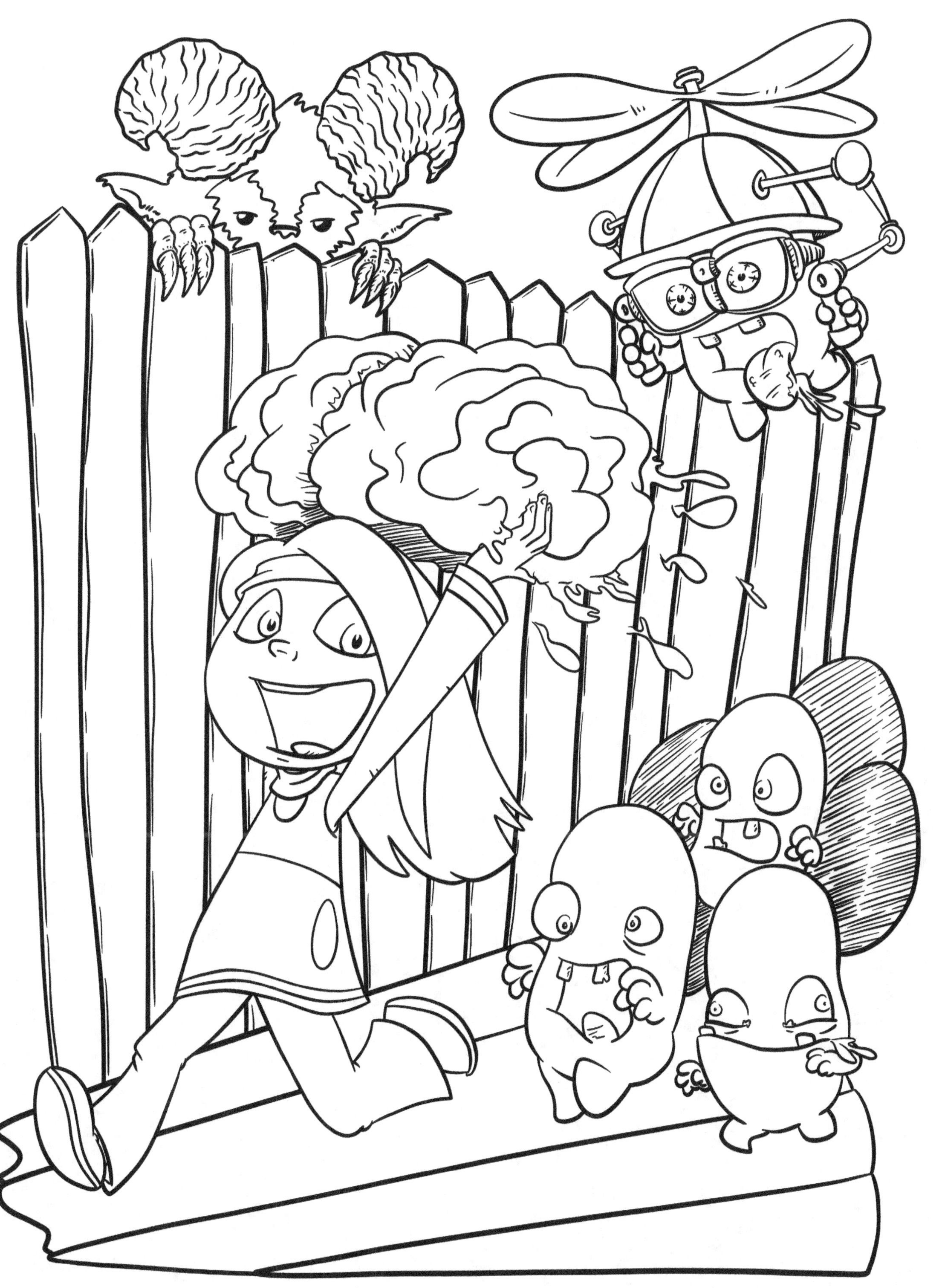

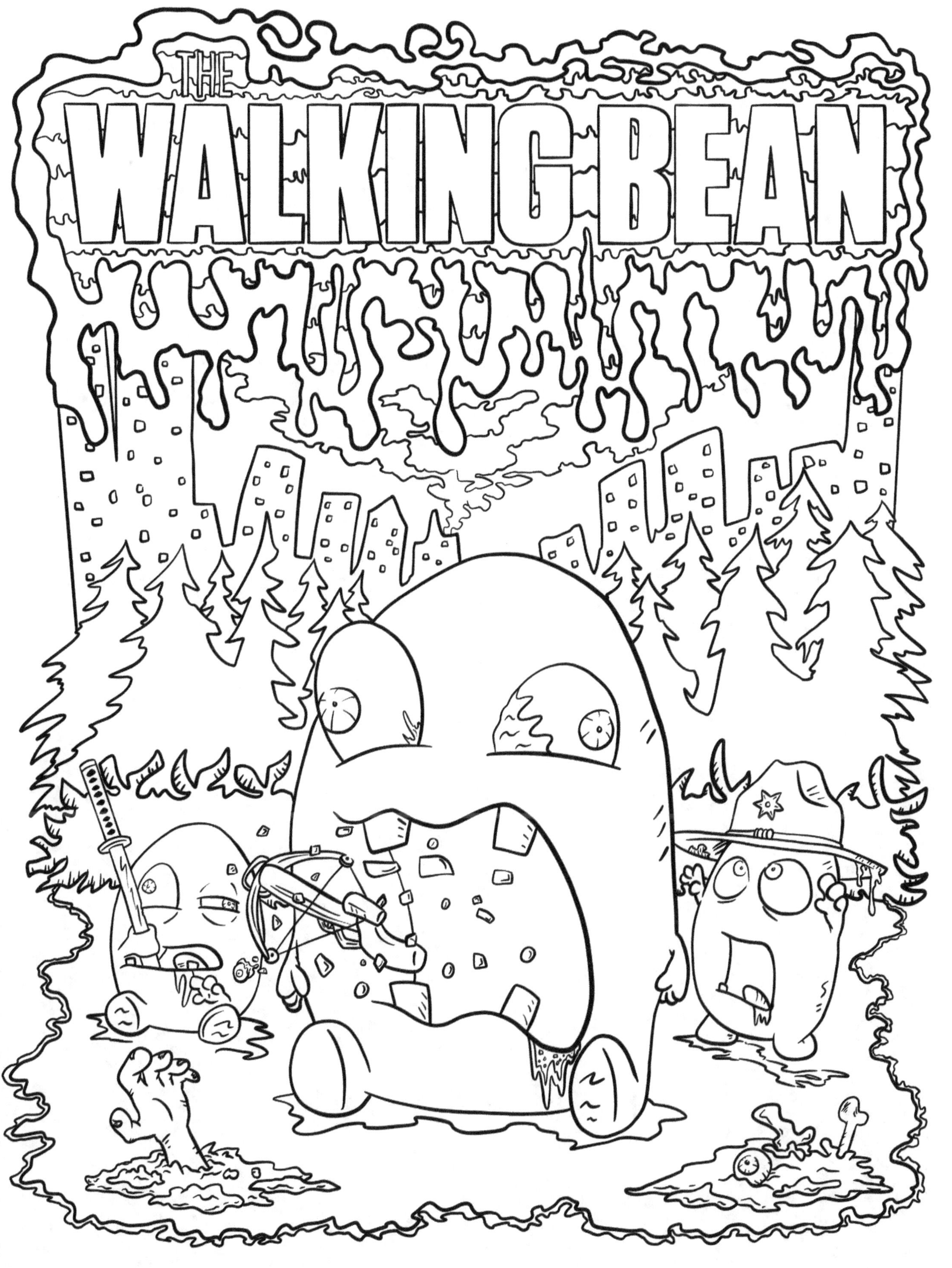
THE WALKING BEAN

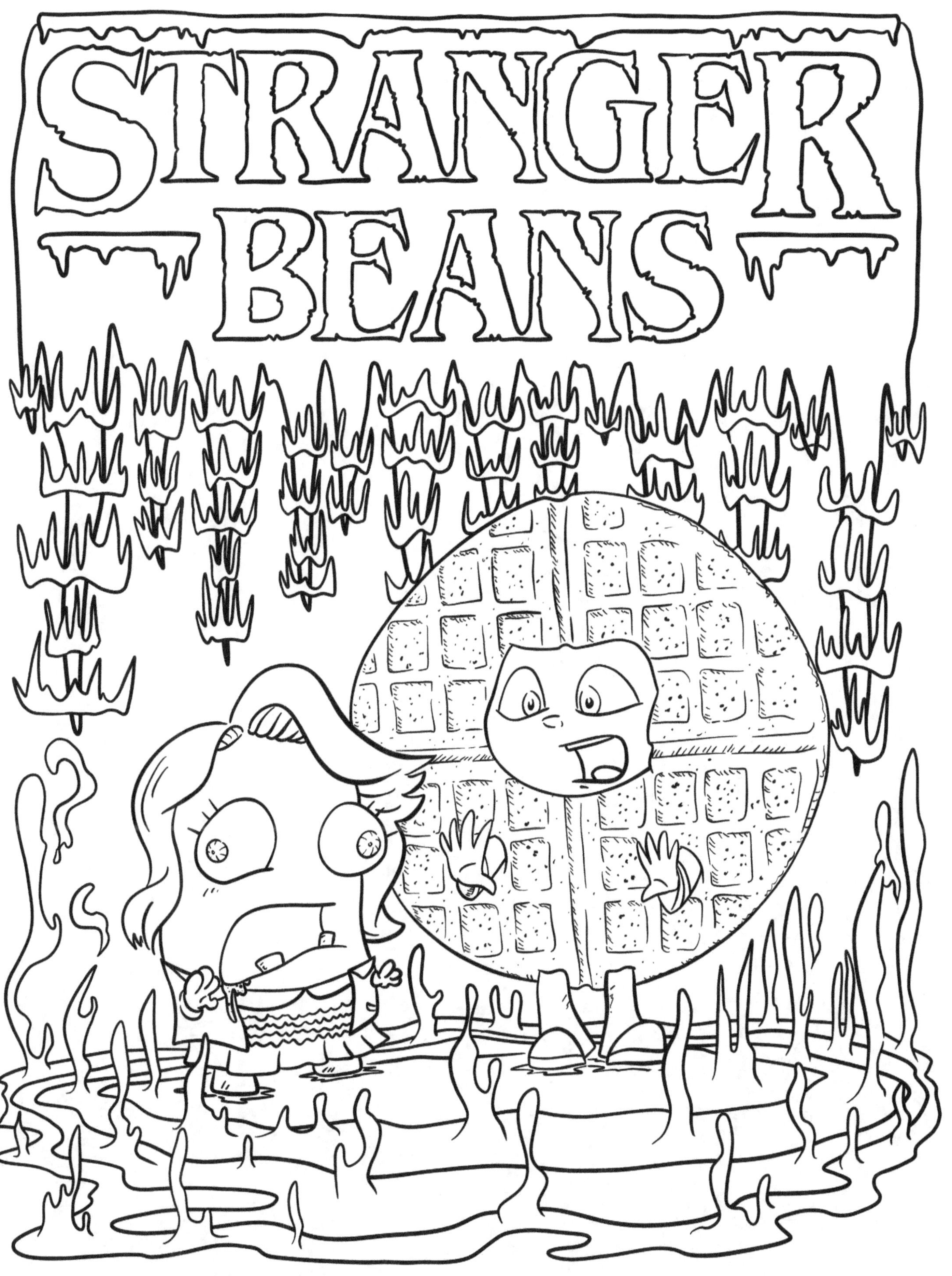

STRANGER
BEANS

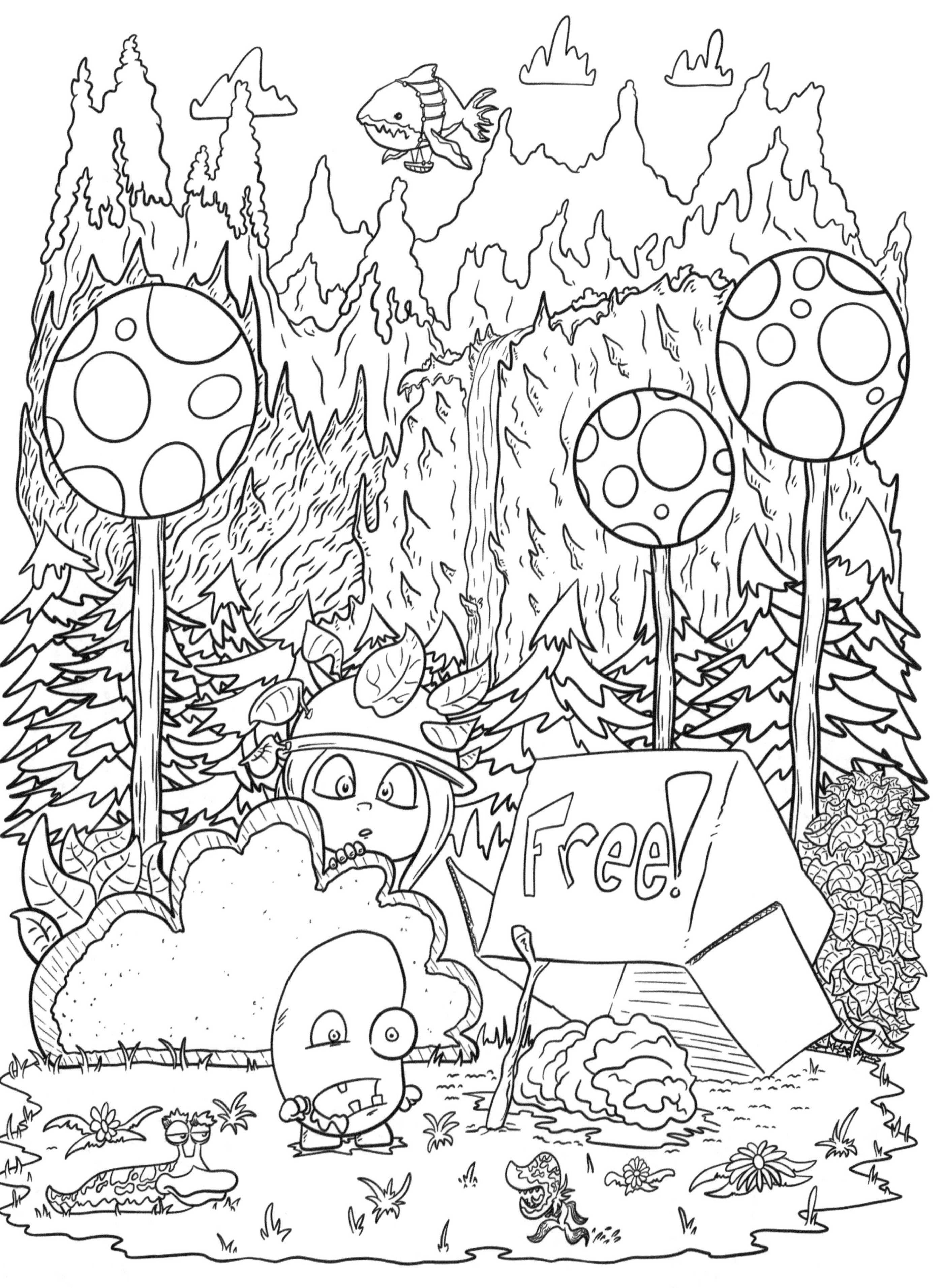
Free!

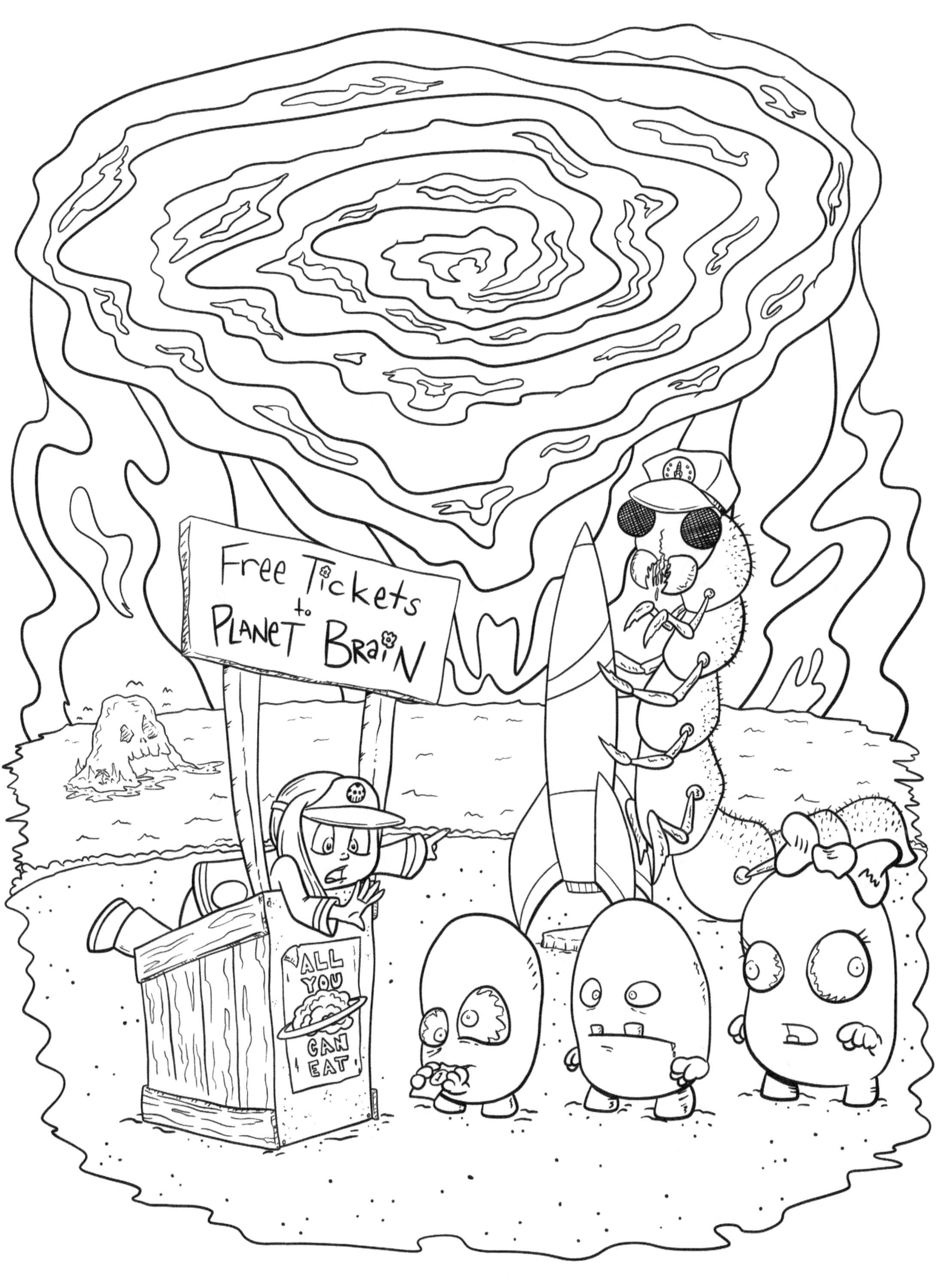

Free Tickets to PLANeT BraiN
ALL YOU CAN EAT

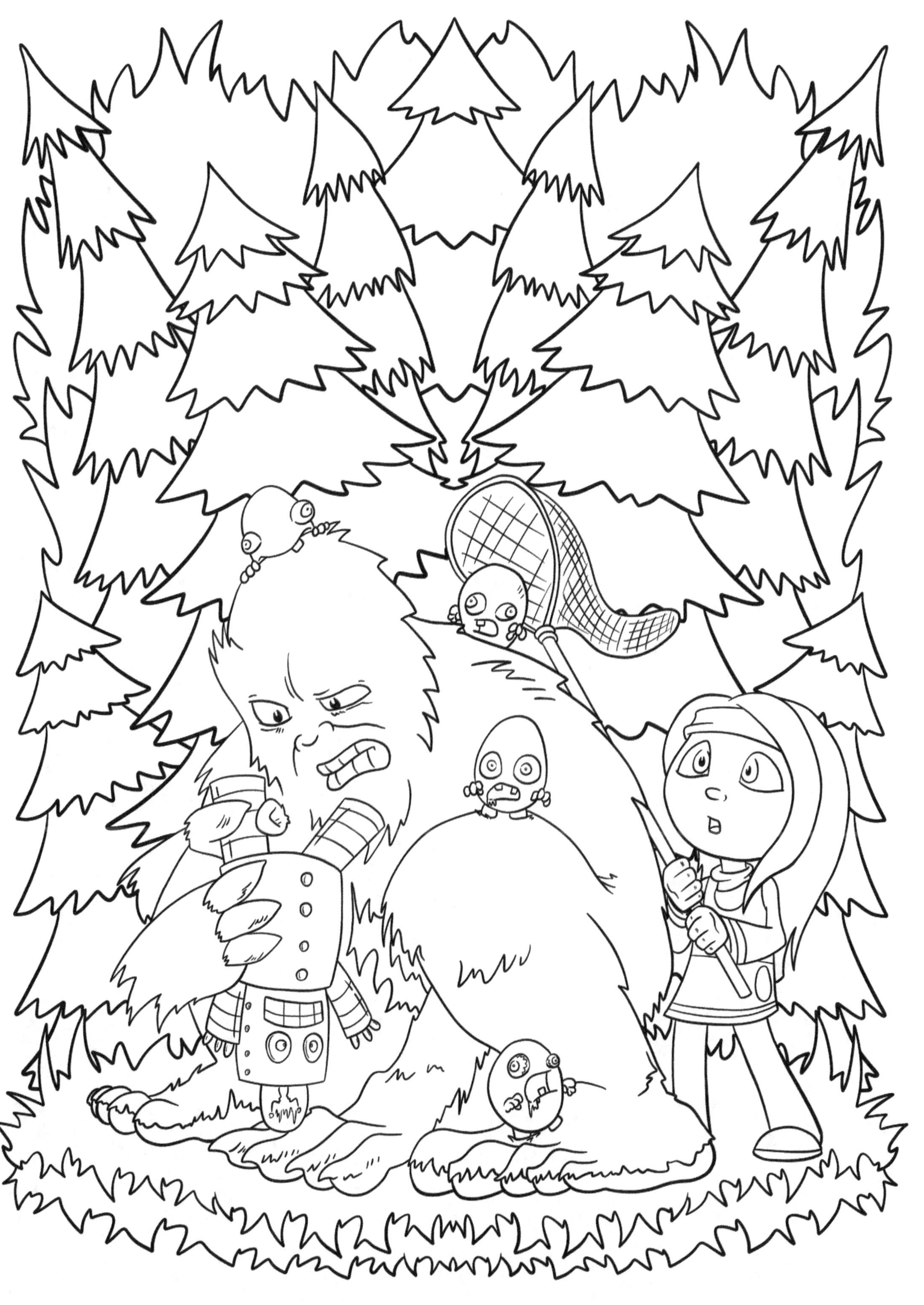

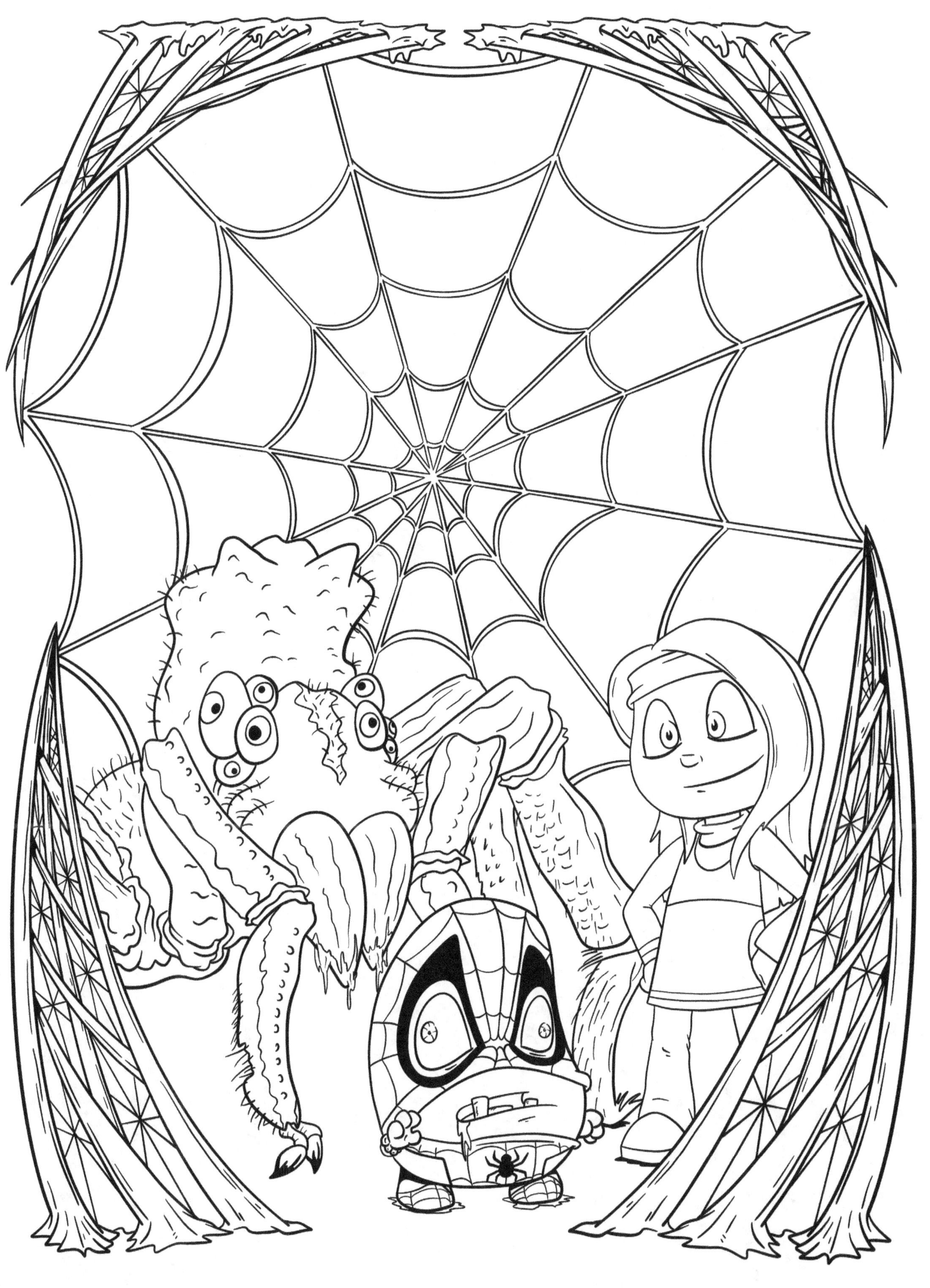

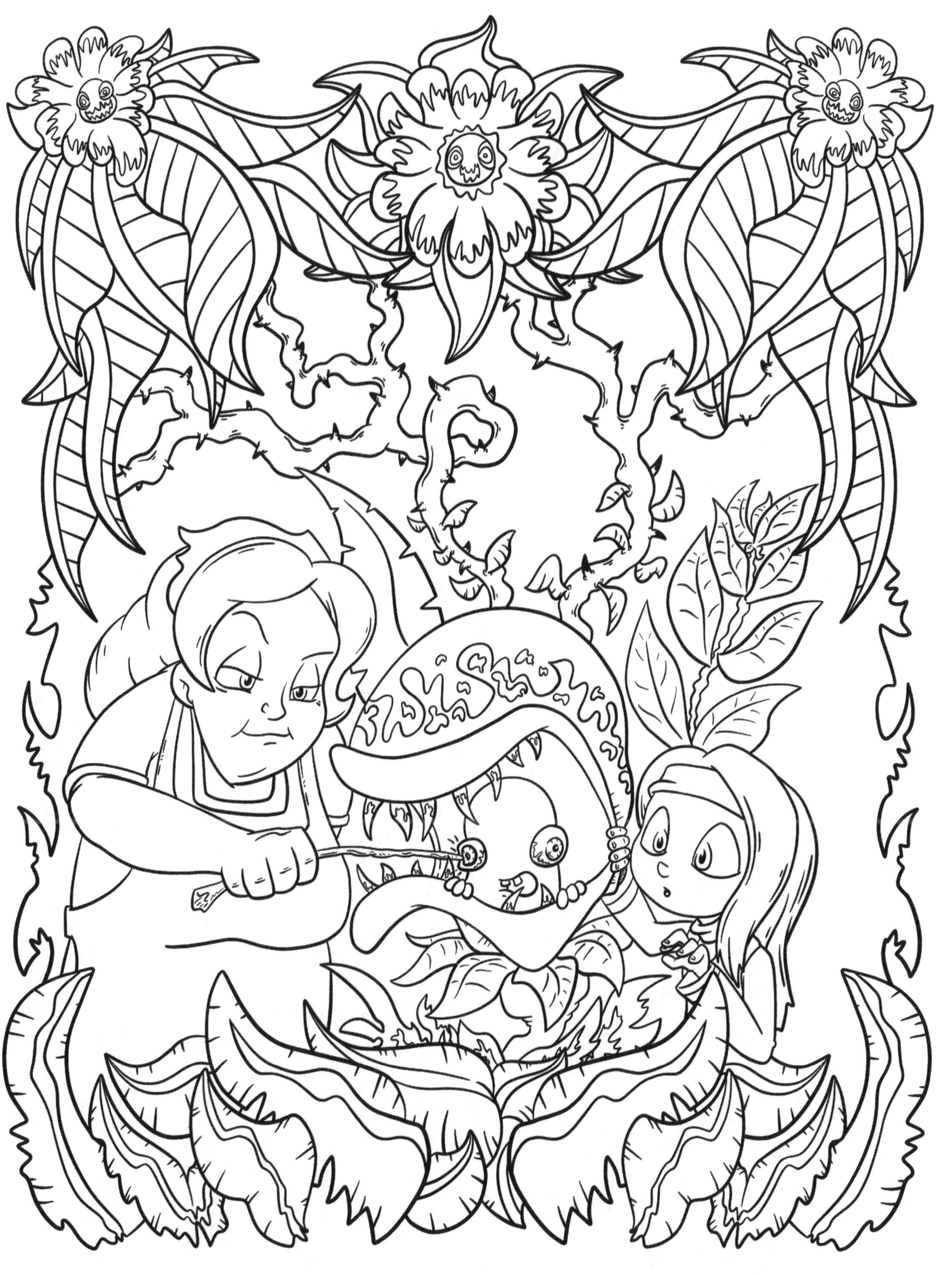

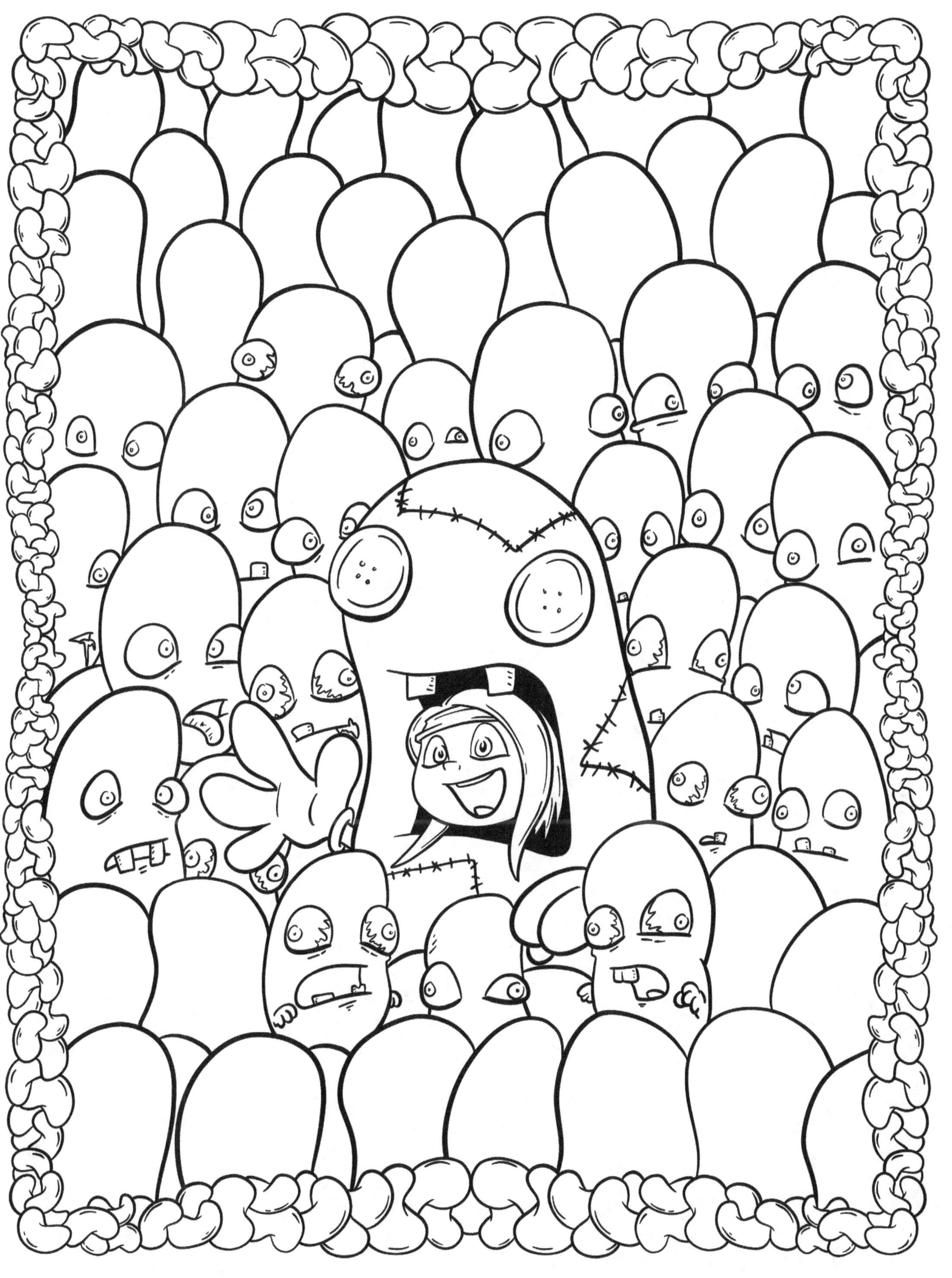

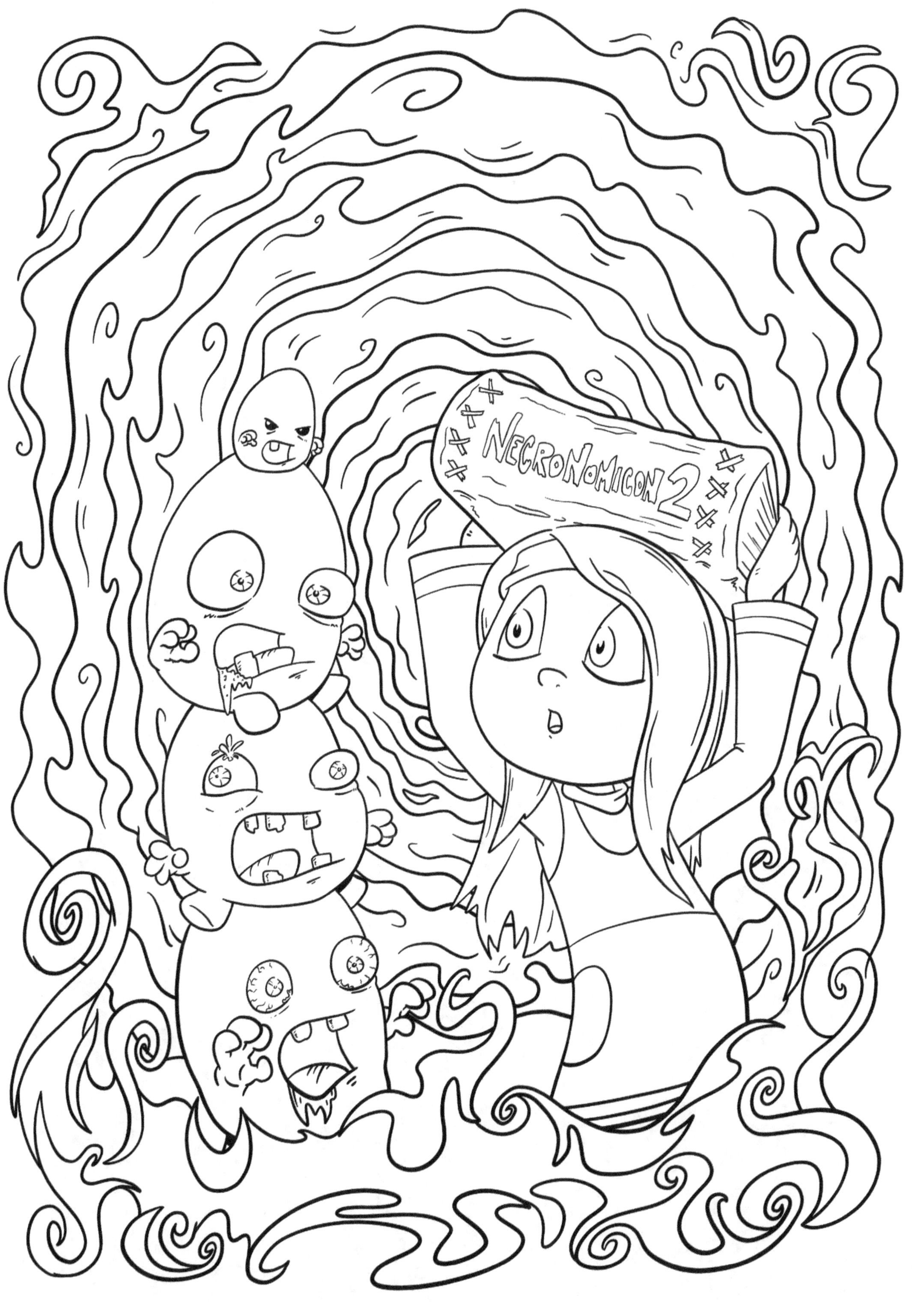

NECRONOMICON 2

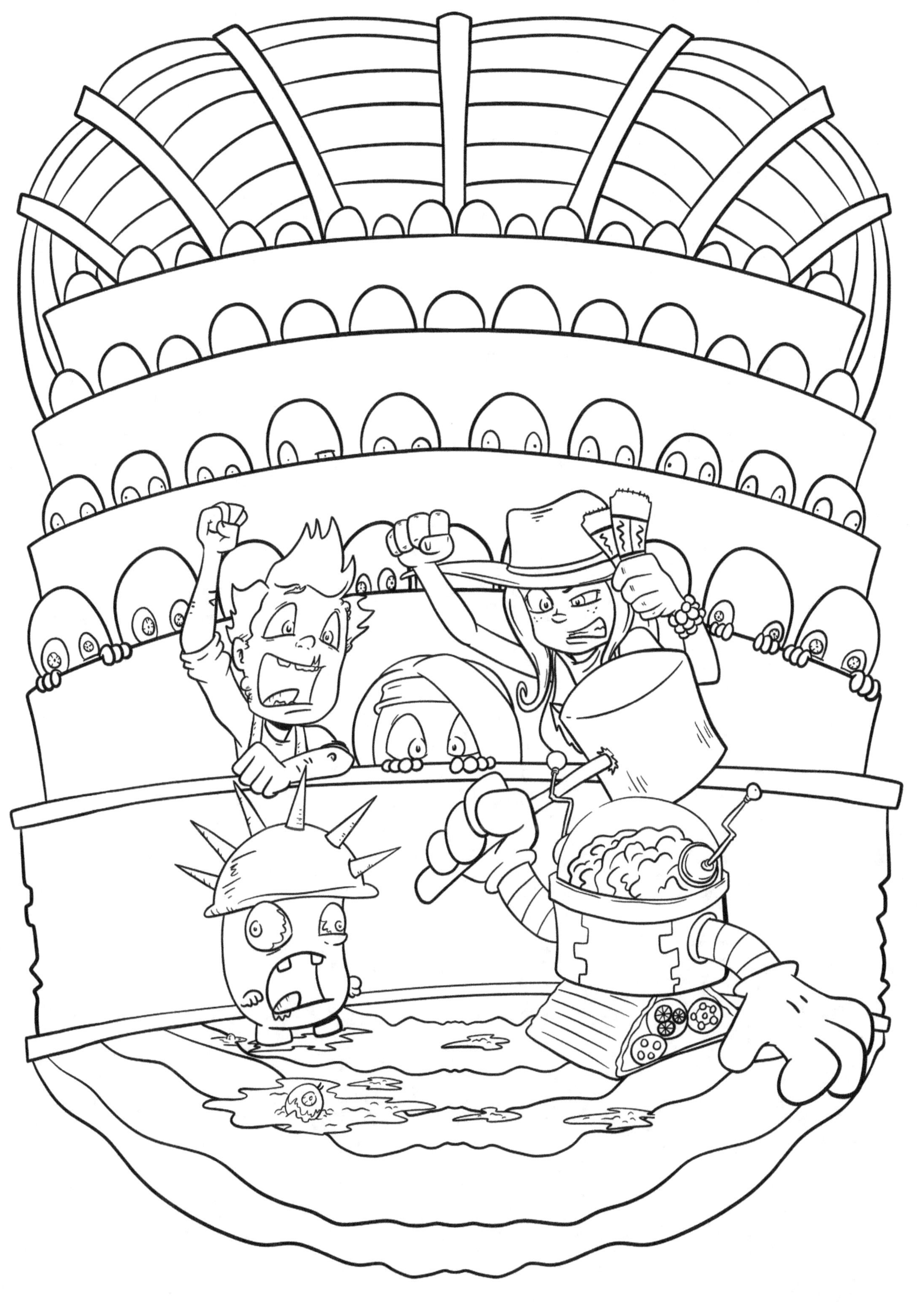

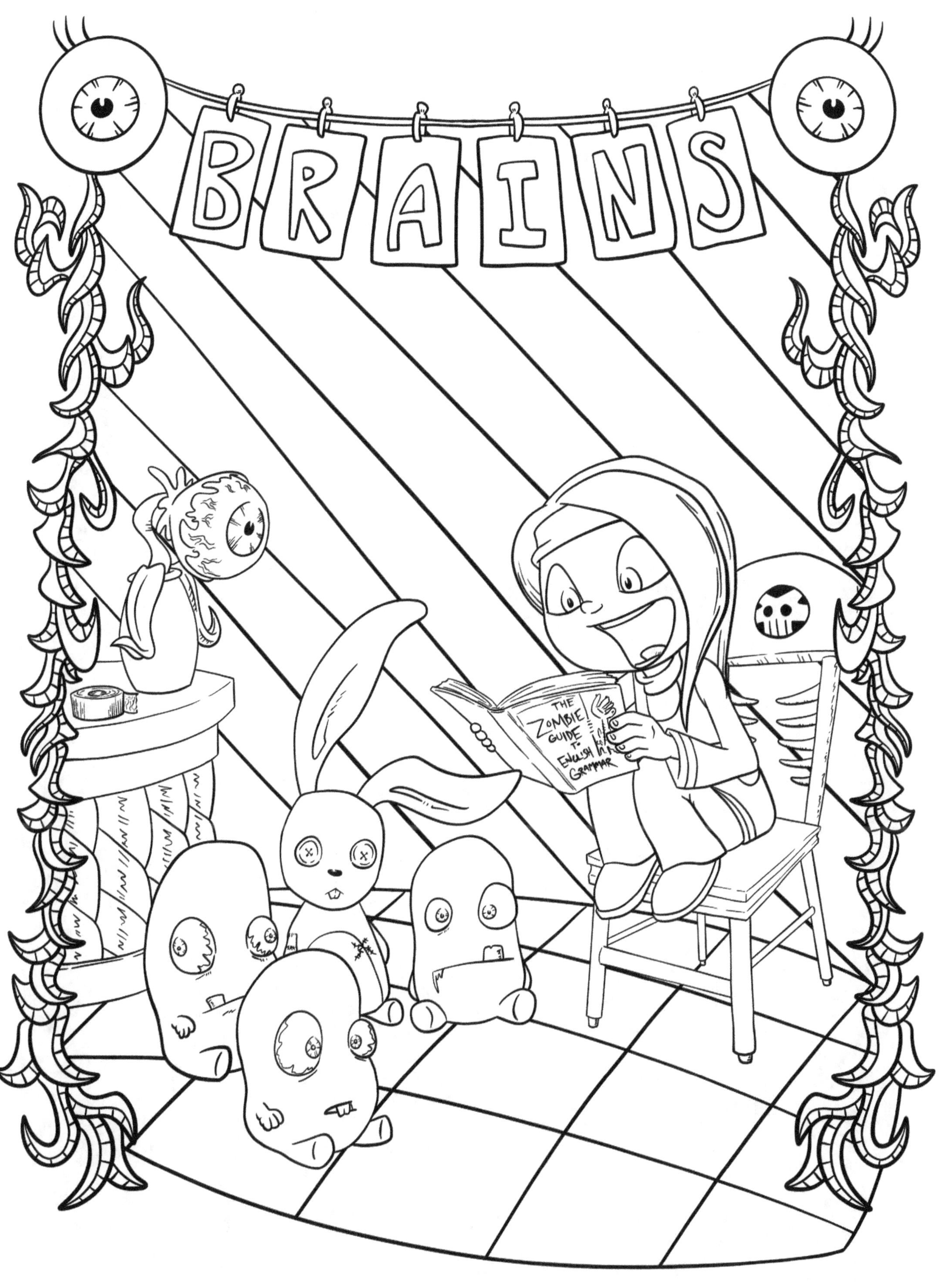

BRAINS
THE ZOMBIE GUIDE TO ENGLISH GRAMMAR

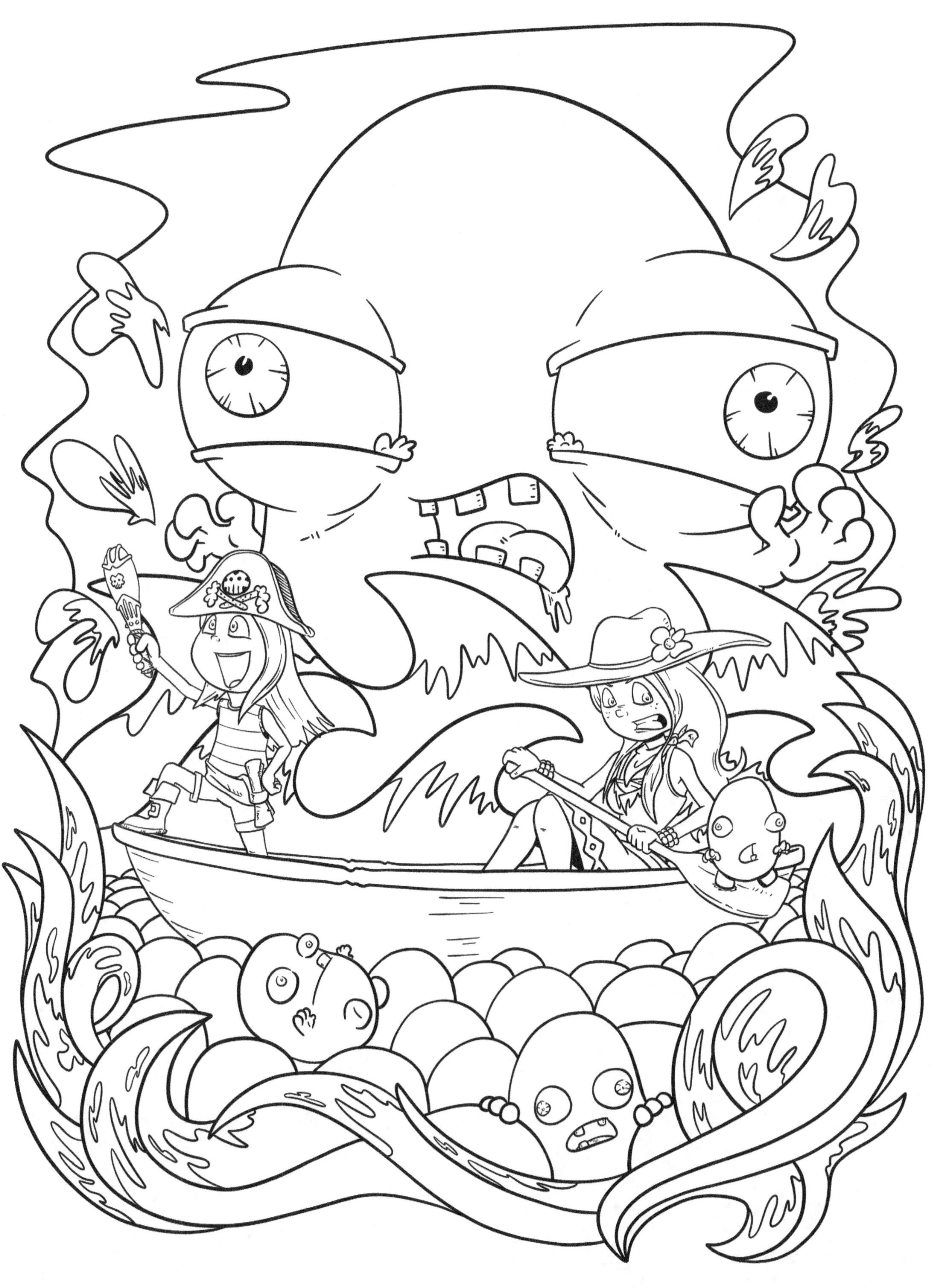

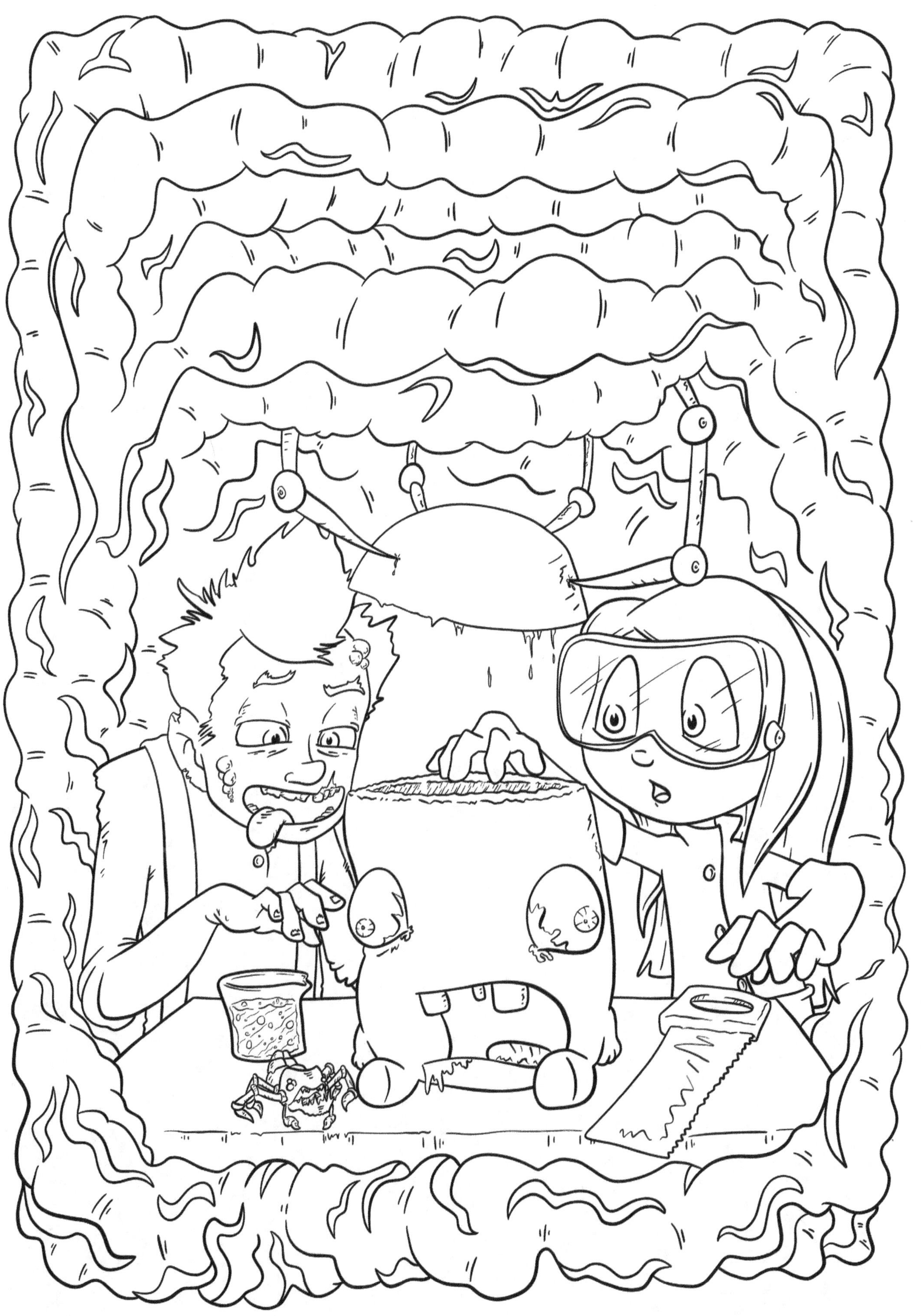

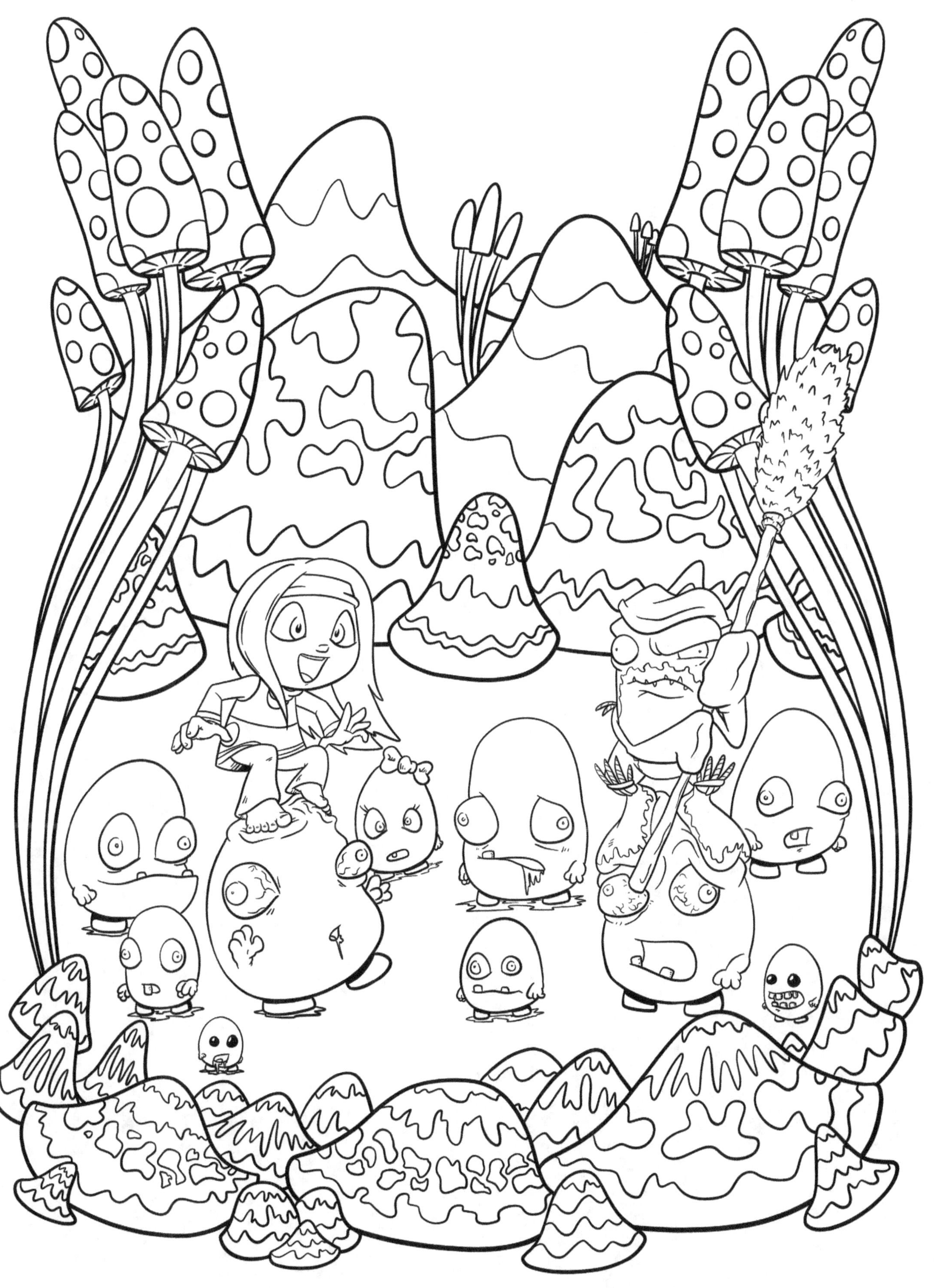

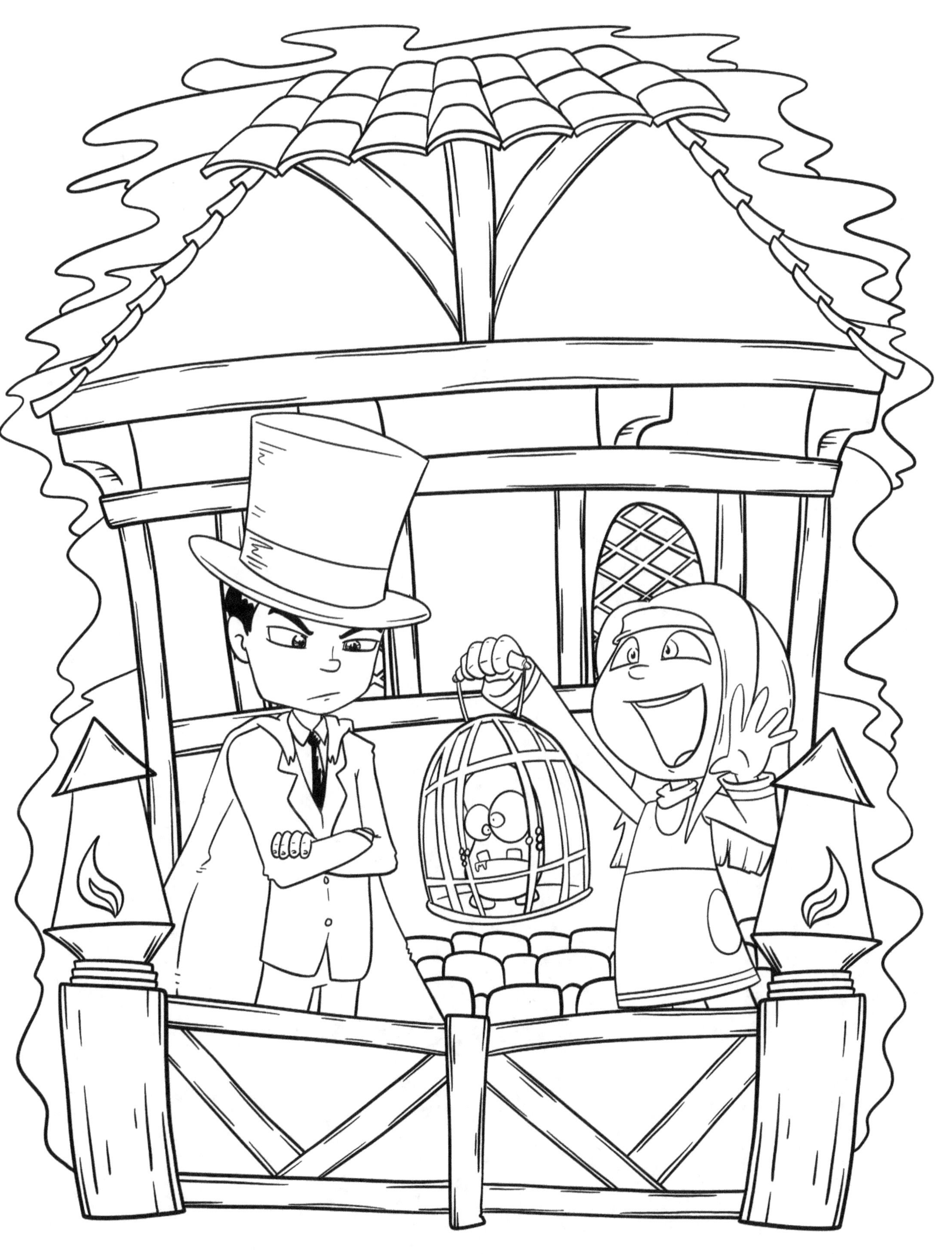

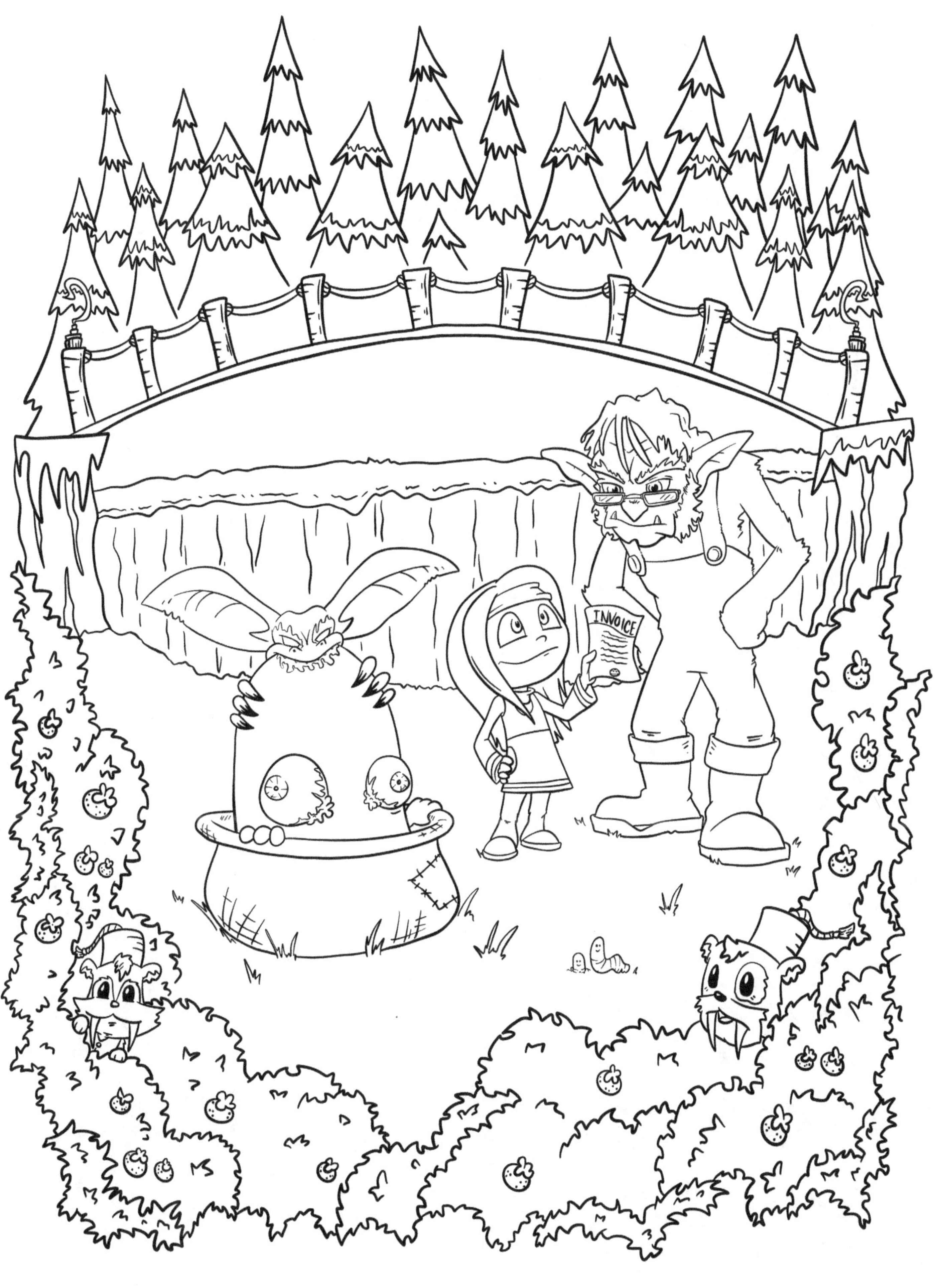

INVOICE

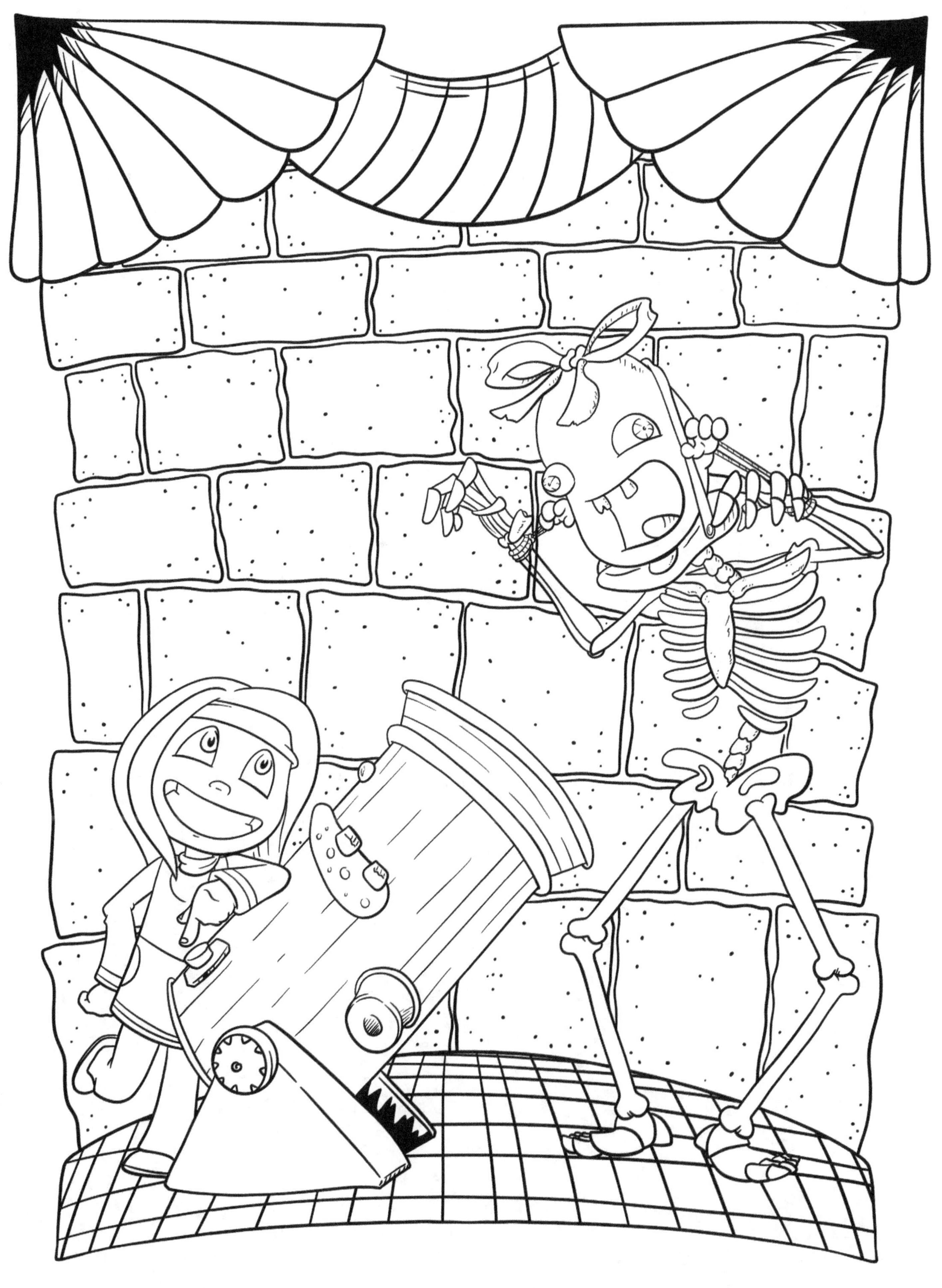

THE ZOMBEAN INVASION IS SPREADING!

IT'S UP TO YOU TO SAVE US ALL!

HUNT DOWN THE ZOMBEANS THROUGHOUT
TIME AND SPACE IN THESE OTHER COLORING BOOKS:

• NIGHT OF THE LIVING ZOMBEANS •

• ZOMBEANS OF HISTORY •

• ZOMBEANS IN SPACE •

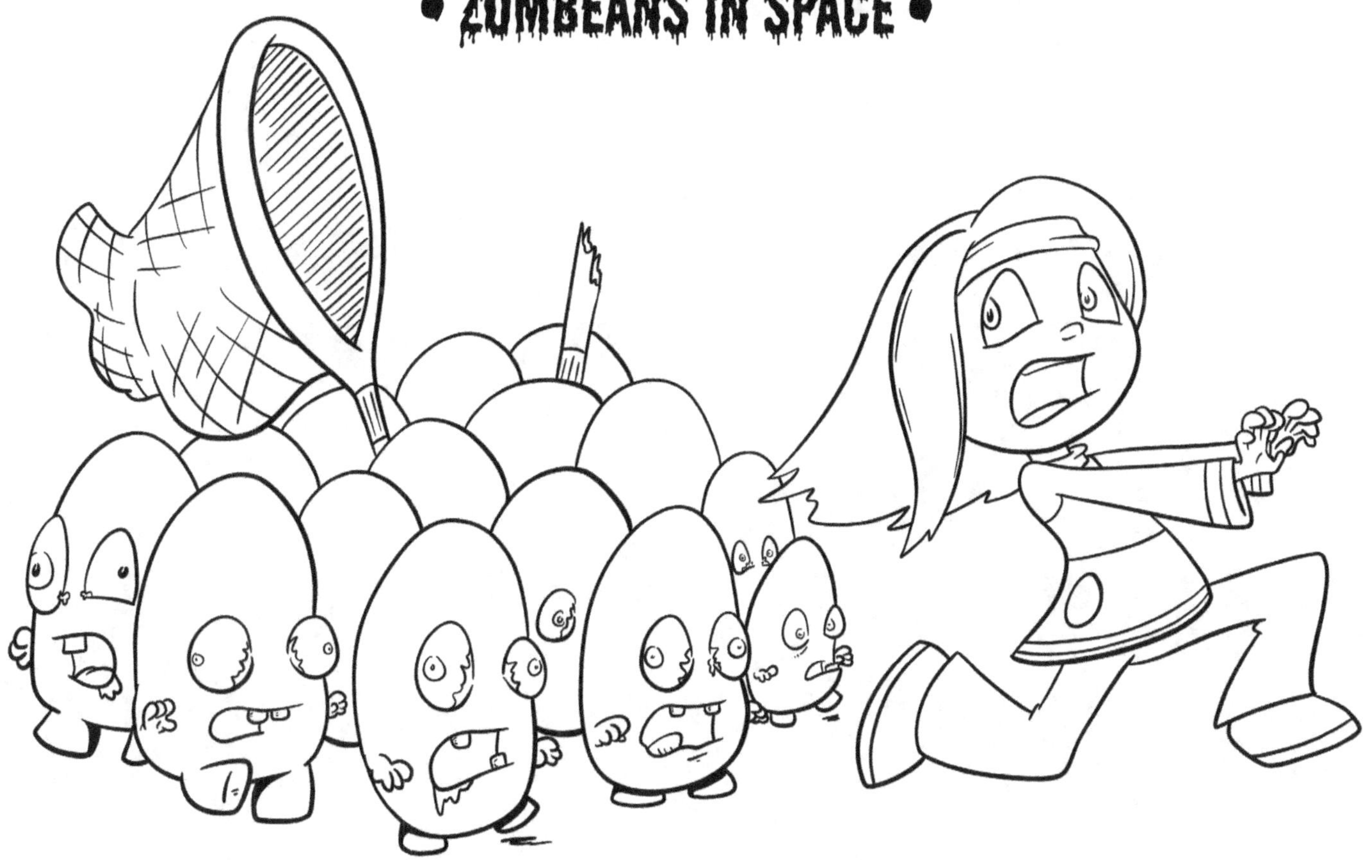

OR ELSE, YOU MAY BE THE NEXT ZOMBIE BEAN...

JOIN THE HORDE!

Get your monsters and more every month
when you sign up on Patreon

• Coloring Books • Stickers • Weird Stuff •
• ZOMBEANIFICATION •

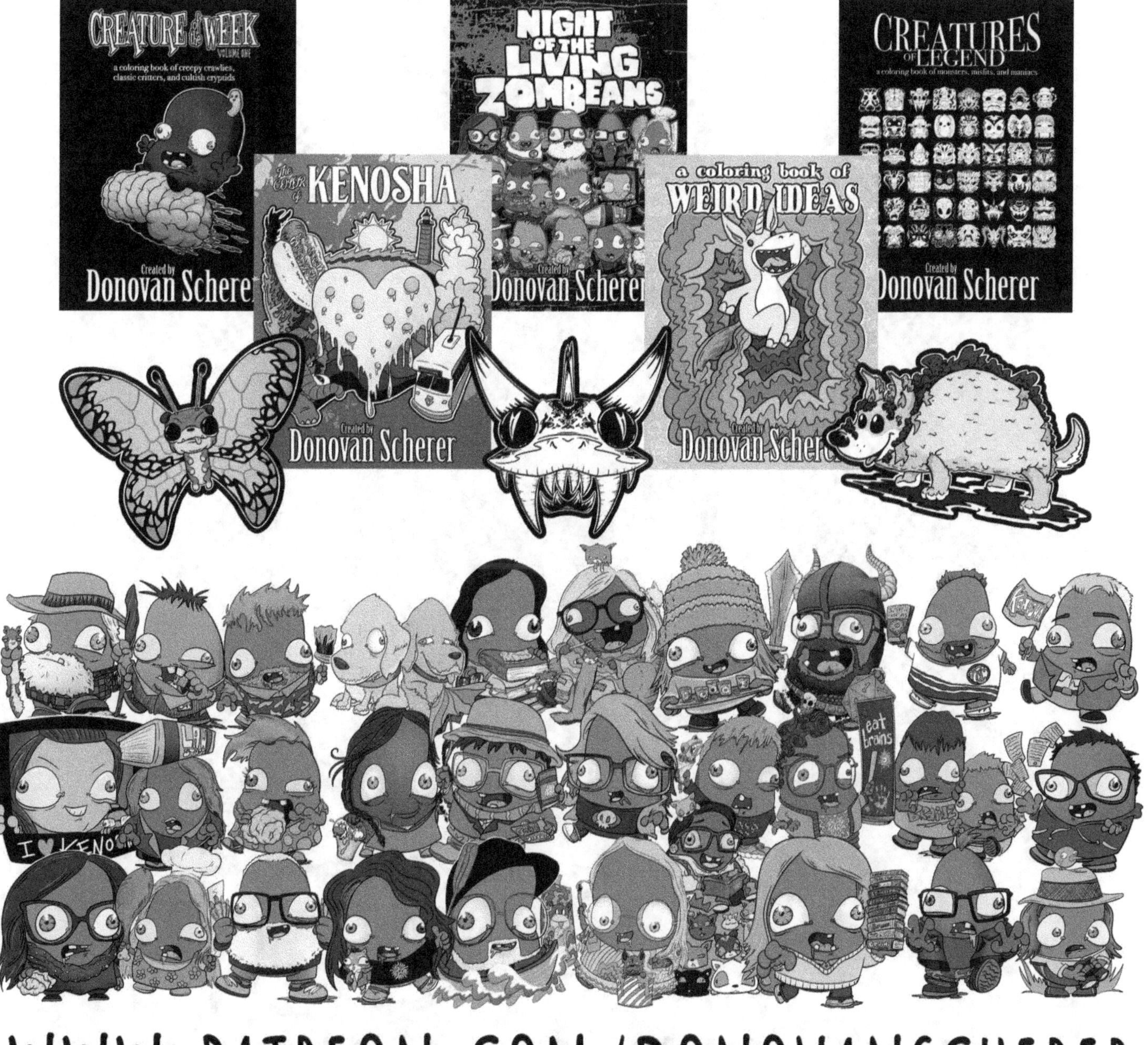

WWW.PATREON.COM/DONOVANSCHERER

VISIT STUDIO MOONFALL

THROUGH THE MAGIC OF SCIENCE!

WWW.MOONFALL360.COM

WANT MORE TO COLOR?

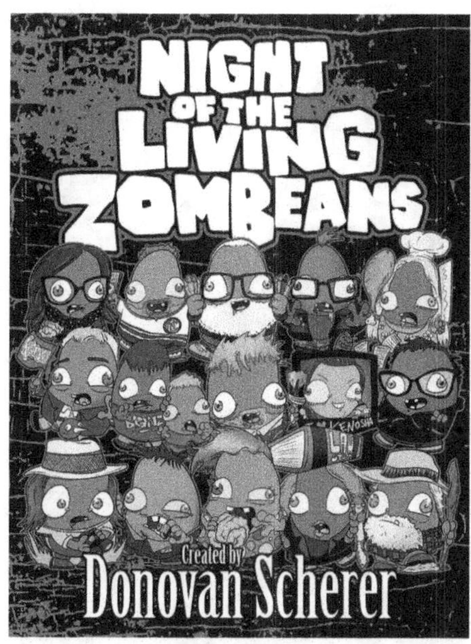

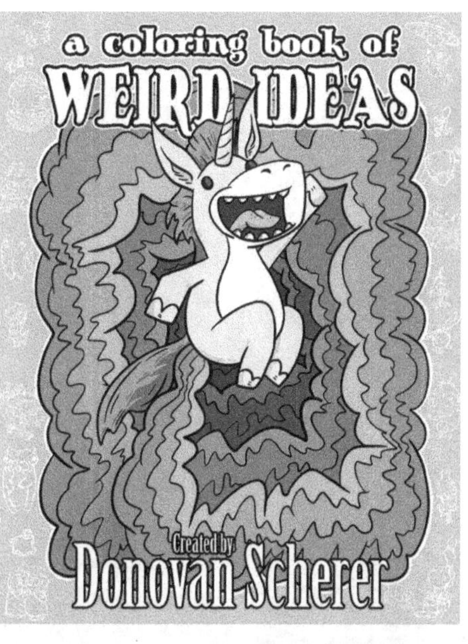

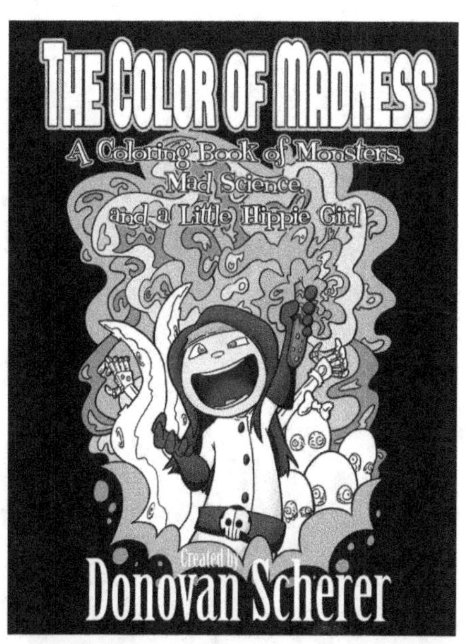

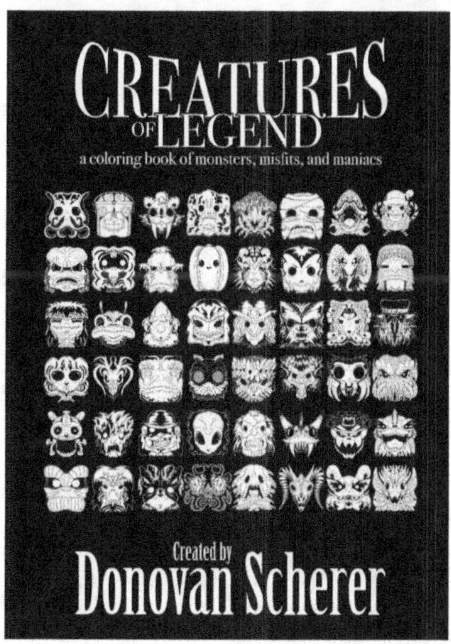

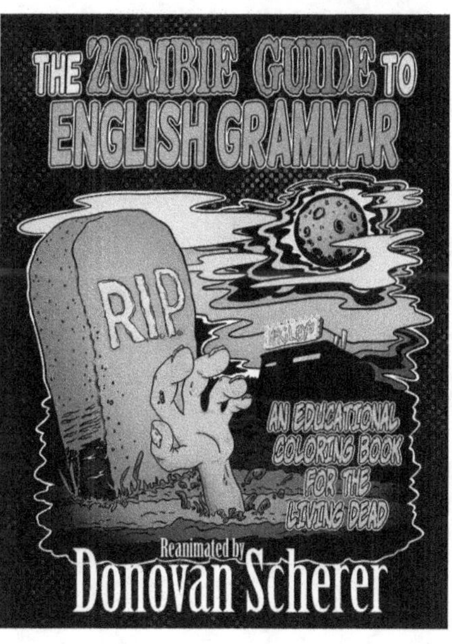

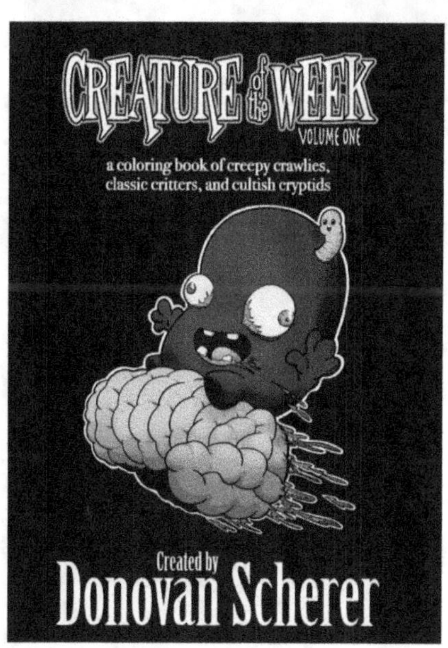

FIND YOUR NEXT COLORING BOOK AND MORE AT:

WWW.STUDIOMOONFALL.COM